"You okay to be in

"I'm fine. But I can't promise these croutons will be in the bowl when you get back." Brooks's daughter grinned and popped a homemade toasted piece of bread in her mouth.

"I feel like that's fair." Vera darted outside and rubbed her arms. It was chilly and the wind seeped through her thin sweater. Thunder clouds rolled in and brought thick gray skies. The air felt wet with impending rain.

When she reached the stable, horses pawed at the doors and neighed. She inhaled the scent of hay and leather and horse manure.

The small A-frame chapel was about a hundred feet away, nestled in a patch of trees. Rows of stained-glass windows on each side. It hadn't been painted white, but was rustic wood. Perfect.

"Brooks! Dinner's—"

A boom splintered the air.

Not thunder.

Dirt surrounding her feet shot into the air.

"Brooks!" Vera dropped to her knees, pulled the weapon she'd kept on her for precaution. But the enemy was unseen. Lurking in the trees.

And she had no cover.

Jessica R. Patch lives in the Mid-South, where she pens inspirational contemporary romance and romantic suspense novels. When she's not hunched over her laptop or going on adventurous trips with willing friends in the name of research, you can find her watching way too much Netflix with her family and collecting recipes for amazing dishes she'll probably never cook. To learn more about Jessica, please visit her at jessicarpatch.com.

Books by Jessica R. Patch

Love Inspired Suspense

Quantico Profilers

Texas Cold Case Threat
Cold Case Killer Profile
Texas Smoke Screen

Cold Case Investigators

Cold Case Takedown
Cold Case Double Cross
Yuletide Cold Case Cover-Up

The Security Specialists

Deep Waters
Secret Service Setup
Dangerous Obsession

Love Inspired Trade

Her Darkest Secret

Visit the Author Profile page at LoveInspired.com for more titles.

TEXAS
SMOKE SCREEN

JESSICA R. PATCH

LOVE INSPIRED SUSPENSE
INSPIRATIONAL ROMANCE

LOVE INSPIRED SUSPENSE

INSPIRATIONAL ROMANCE

ISBN-13: 978-1-335-58819-7

Texas Smoke Screen

Copyright © 2022 by Jessica R. Patch

Recycling programs
for this product may
not exist in your area.

For questions and comments about the quality of this book, please contact us
at CustomerService@Harlequin.com.

Love Inspired
22 Adelaide St. West, 41st Floor
Toronto, Ontario M5H 4E3, Canada
www.LoveInspired.com

Printed in U.S.A.

The Spirit of the Lord God is upon me;
because the Lord hath anointed me to preach
good tidings unto the meek; he hath sent me to bind up
the brokenhearted, to proclaim liberty to the captives,
and the opening of the prison to them that are bound;
To proclaim the acceptable year of the Lord, and the
day of vengeance of our God; to comfort all that mourn;
To appoint unto them that mourn in Zion, to give unto
them beauty for ashes, the oil of joy for mourning,
the garment of praise for the spirit of heaviness;
that they might be called trees of righteousness,
the planting of the Lord, that he might be glorified.
—*Isaiah* 61:1-3

To anyone with scars. Inside or out.
You are brave and beautiful.

Special thanks:

To my incredible agent.
Thank you for your wisdom and friendship.

To my awesome editor, Shana Asaro.
You keep making my books better.

To Susan Tuttle, who, as always, brainstorms like a boss
and tells me when I'm off the mark and
always makes time for me. Your friendship is golden.

To Jodie Bailey for always being there
to give me great distractions, pep talks
and reasons to laugh when I really want to cry.

ONE

Soot and flecks of ash coated Special Agent Vera Gilmore's tongue and stabbed her gag reflex as panic galloped through her chest like a wild stallion speeding across a Texas desert. Coming to Serenity Canyon had been a mistake. But when Brooks Brawley had called her, telling her people had been burned alive, she'd been too shocked to say no. She had the ability to aid him, and she wanted to.

Over twenty years had passed since she'd laid eyes on her former college boyfriend. After graduation, he'd chosen to return to his small West Texas town where he was now the lead homicide detective, and Vera had pursued a career in the FBI. She'd been with the BAU—Behavioral Analysis Unit—in Quantico for the past six years.

Life had forked between her and Brooks, led them down opposite roads to new people and new lives. Lives where new dreams had been birthed and the future had been full of possibilities, until they weren't anymore. Tragedy and death had stolen from them both. Many nights, Vera had awakened to nightmares, slicked in sweat, hair matted to her face, and no one to hold her close and comfort her. Not anymore. Only hollow remnants of a life that had been good and well-lived remained buried under the ash of Danny's death.

She fanned her face. January in Texas felt like October in Quantico, Virginia. Mid to upper sixties during the day and fifties in the evening, but the memories burned hot and flushed her cheeks. Even now she could feel the flames licking up her body, melting her flesh and stealing Danny away. Eight years since she'd tried to rescue him from the blazing inferno of their home. Eight years of widowhood. And she was only forty-one.

If only she'd blown out that candle before they'd gone to bed.

She shuddered and refocused on the case at hand and the latest crime scene—charred remains of a horse stable on a small ranch. Rubble and ashes littered the floor. Glancing up through the gaping hole in the roof, she saw the sky tinted in orange and pinks as the sun made its rest for the night.

The stable popped and cracked. But Keegan

Lane, the fire lieutenant, had said the structure was secure enough, though he wouldn't recommend taking up homestead. He was walking around the outside of the building, looking through debris. It had been two decades since she'd seen him too. He'd been Brooks's childhood best friend. She'd met him a few times when she'd come home with Brooks for a holiday or during the summer.

"Vera, I meant what I said," Keegan reminded as he poked his head inside. "Take your time but hurry up. Nothing is absolute."

Wasn't that the truth.

Brooks had remained outside the stable, allowing her time to go inside alone, examine the damage and, if she had to guess, to give her time to deal with her emotions. It had a been a long time since she'd stood within a building eaten by fire and it had brought back old, terrible and painful memories.

Brooks had always been discerning and thoughtful. With a mom who had suffered from MS, he'd known the responsibility of helping to care for a loved one and see to their needs. She'd passed not long after they parted ways romantically.

The sound of feet shuffling and kicking away rubble drew her attention. Brooks's imposing frame cast a long shadow as he stood with his hands in his dark denim pockets. He'd always been a big guy with a velvety baritone voice that could lull one to comfort or intimidate. His thick black hair wasn't showing signs of age just yet and was cut short with a few trendy spikes up front. Only the crinkles around his intense blue eyes showed he was on his way to the midforties.

"What are you thinking?" he asked.

She sighed and rubbed the puckers on her right wrist. The long sleeves, slacks and her shoulder-length hair could hide most of the scars, except the ones on her hands. Unless she wore gloves, and it wasn't cold enough for those. "The killer let the horses out before setting the fire. Could be to create the diversion so the victim would come out of the house. Could be simply because he's an animal lover."

Brooks opened his mouth and Vera held up her hand. She knew what he was going to say.

"I say *he* because most arsonists are men. Women make up a small percentage—so I'm not ruling out a woman, but for sake of conversation, I'm going with a male. Young. White. He may have a record for earlier offenses, though less dramatic than this latest string, and probably not homicides involved. I can't say much more until I talk to your friend Tracey." She surveyed the stable. "She's clearly the key."

Brooks's worried brow revealed his very real concern for his late wife's best friend. An investigative reporter for the local news station, Tracey had been anonymously called concerning all three fires in the past six months. He'd found out her cell phone number and wanted her to know first. "I just wish I knew why."

Lieutenant Lane entered the stable. His sandy-brown hair *was* showing signs of age and his leathery skin revealed he spent most of his time outdoors when not working at the small Serenity Canyon fire department. "The MO is the same. Basic Molotov cocktail. All anyone needs to do is google it and they can learn how to make one. Flammable liquid, a bottle and a rag. Light it. Toss it. Torch it. In this case, it's gasoline and a glass soda bottle."

Brooks heaved a sigh. "Easy to buy, hard to trace. Just like the burner phone he's used to call Tracey. Not just hard—impossible."

Vera hadn't had a full briefing yet. Just an initial call from Brooks with a heartfelt plea to help. "Do the victims connect with one another?"

Brooks shook his head. "Not with each other that we can find. Just a slight connection to Tracey, minus our first victim. Stranger camping near Big Bend National Park in his camper truck. It was set on fire in the night. Second vic had ties to Tracey. Intern at the news station. She'd recently been hired. Tracey didn't know her well. No one did. But this last one...it's personal." Brooks balled a fist. "She's my daughter's social studies teacher and soccer coach. Tracey and she had become friends since she'd been taking Katie to practices and helped with picking her up from school. The kid's a mess." He heaved a sigh and raked a hand through his hair.

Hmm...maybe it wasn't a purposely trendy hairdo as she'd first thought, but spikes of hair due to stress-combing.

"I'm sorry," Vera said. Loss was always a mess. "I'd like to talk to Tracey. He's called her personally with her private cell number and he's choosing people she's connected to. She's important to him. I need to know why."

"Of course."

"Look, y'all. I need to go," Keegan said. "I wouldn't stick around too much longer. I'm not saying you aren't safe but I'm not saying you are either." Lieutenant Lane nodded to Vera. "It's good to see you again. Sorry it's under these circumstances." He slapped Brooks on the back. "I'll call you later."

He strode toward the white truck with the Serenity Canyon fire department sticker on the side.

"I never pegged him as one to go into the fire department. He was always in trouble, if I remember right."

Brooks chuckled. "He's a good egg. Best man at my wedding. CeCe threatened him with his life if he played a prank during the ceremony. She just knew he was going to set off the fire alarm." He chuckled at the sweet memory.

Danny had been a jokester too. She actually missed evenings when he'd been doing the dishes and spontaneously sprayed her with the sink nozzle, turning the kitchen into a watery disaster. She'd scolded him, but secretly loved his playful side.

"He sounds fun. Is he married?"

"You interested?" he teased.

She gave him the get-real look.

Brooks shook his head. "Nah. I don't know that he'll ever settle down. Did go out for a brief time with Tracey. CeCe was forever the matchmaker. But that didn't stick. And then Tracey met someone else." He shrugged. "So he's available and a catch."

"The only thing I want to catch is this killer."

"Me too."

She paused before moving on with the investigation, affected by his mention of his late wife. While she'd sent flowers to the funeral, she hadn't personally called or given her condo-

lences. Maybe she should have. "I'm sorry for
your loss, Brooks. I'm sure CeCe was a wonderful woman." From what little Vera knew, CeCe
Brawley had been a speech pathologist and the
leader of their church's women's ministry. She'd
died in a tragic car accident coming home from
a women's retreat in the Texas Hill Country two
years ago. Brooks's loss wasn't simply tender;
it was fresh.

"She was," he said in a low timbre. He inhaled deeply and scanned the stable. "Anything
else here speak to you?"

The killer had lured out Adrianna Montega,
the soccer coach, when he'd let the horses loose.
Once she'd entered the stable, he'd barricaded
her inside, but they were unsure with what as
it had been less than twenty-four hours since
the crime was perpetrated. After imprisoning
her, he'd tossed the Molotov cocktail through
the open loft window, which was stocked with
hay bales. The fire had ignited fast and been
furious.

Vera knew firsthand how rapidly a fire
spread. Like a ravenous monster with an insatia-
ble appetite. One little candle flame had turned
into a blaze, consuming their home in a matter
of minutes. Vera didn't have to imagine what
went through Adrianna's mind or the fear that
overtook her. She knew it well. Since the fire,

she couldn't help but look for exits upon entering every store or establishment. She detested confined spaces and she refused to ever live in a two-story home again. They might have made it out had it not been for the time it took to get an already unconscious man down the stairs.

"We're about to lose light." His cell phone rang. "It's Katie. I need to take this."

She smiled and motioned him to take the call. "I'm about done. Go on. I'll catch up." Vera wanted one more look around. She had two more crime scenes to visit, but not tonight. She needed to try to slide into the killer's mind. She knew the how. She needed the why. What was his ultimate goal? What did he want the world to know? Or was this more about Tracey Tisdale than the news she reported? She was a focal point for sure.

Vera took slow, measured steps outside the stable, studying the distance from the ranch house where the victim had lived. According to Brooks, Adrianna had inherited it from her grandfather and was preparing it to sell.

Brooks also owned a ranch, but she hadn't seen it yet. Earlier he'd met her in baggage claim at the airport and the moment she'd seen him, a flutter in her chest had unsettled her. It had been such a long time since she'd felt that for anyone, but it had brought back that swooping, heady feeling she used to experience around him over two decades ago.

They'd been kids.

A lot of life and time had passed. She'd grown. Matured. And yet he still evoked that feeling. Not only had it startled her, it scared her. Vera didn't want to feel flutters for a man—any man. Flutters led to feelings, and feelings led to commitment, which led to marriage and intimacy...and that terrified her most.

When Danny died, she didn't believe she'd ever be attracted to another man, but after three years, she was. She'd accepted a date with a federal agent. One date had led to four. But Vera was good at her job and she'd noticed his behavior. He chose to sit on her left side, hold her left hand. She'd hoped it was paranoia. Reading too much into it. But after a couple of months, he'd finally admitted he was struggling with her scars.

He was struggling.

She knew after the fire she'd changed. But it was in that moment the reality struck her. She was not the woman she once was and never would be. Not to her. Not to the opposite sex. The crushing blow and humiliation had sealed her resolve. No one would reject her again. She wouldn't allow it. Even if it meant being alone and lonely.

She slowly circled the stable. The killer must have come on foot. The only way to this spot was up the main drive, past the house. Adrianna would have heard a vehicle, seen headlights—driving in the pitch-black would have been too dangerous. No, he'd parked somewhere, knowing he'd have plenty of time to return to wherever he'd stashed his vehicle. He'd had nothing heavy to haul. Only a soda bottle full of gasoline and a lighter.

The stable was a long rectangle with two sliding doors on opposite ends. Overhead was a large loft with windows above the doors. He would have only needed to open one stable door plus each stall door to get the horses outside. Once Adrianna entered, he would have closed the door then barricaded it with something that wouldn't burn away and give her the chance to escape. Once the bottle was tossed through the window above, the fire would have ignited the hay in the loft and the stable would have burned quickly.

Using her cell phone flashlight, she reentered the stable and shone the beam on the half-eaten loft. He might have athletic ability. Maybe played baseball or softball. It would have taken a good aim and arm to ensure it went through the window.

Rustling drew her attention. Brooks must have returned.

Cold chills swept down her spine and she paused. "Brooks?" she asked softly.

A crack like a monster tree limb splitting from a storm strike startled her and she shot a glance upward just in time to see a huge broken and charred beam barrel toward her.

She shrieked and bolted, but she wasn't fast enough. The heavy wood clipped her.

A searing pain shot up her leg and she cried out as she fell, smacking her head on something hard. Stars burst before her eyes as she caught faint sight of a dark figure running from the stable.

Then blackness engulfed her.

Vera's bloodcurdling scream sent his nerves on edge and Brooks abruptly ended the phone call as he flew to the stable, tripping over brush.

An eerie silence shoved a mountain of fear into his throat and kicked up his pulse.

"Vera!"

Nothing.

Heart jackhammering against his ribs, he burst into the sooty stable, using his cell flashlight to find her as he called her name.

Again, no answer.

He should have been more alert, more watchful. He'd heard the crack, assumed it was a limb. He'd already been second-guessing himself since he'd called Vera and all but begged her to fly out to profile the serial arsonist committing homicides in his small town. Knowing about her husband's tragic death and Vera's valiant effort to save him, which had badly burned and nearly killed her as well, had given him some hesitation, but he was desperate to catch this killer who was wreaking havoc on his community.

Already he felt selfish and insensitive but Vera's reputation for behavioral analysis was stellar and he knew personally how good she was. If she was hurt...

Ahead, near the west side of the stable, he spotted her lying in a heap, a large charred beam lying across her legs. Racing to her side, he dropped on his knees and felt for a pulse.

Thank You, Lord. There was one. She'd hit her head though. Blood splotched her hairline. He called 9-1-1 then propped up his phone for light. Using both hands, he put all his muscle into lifting the heavy beam from her legs. He dropped it with a thud, raising the settled ashes into the air and into his lungs.

He said her name through a cough, but she didn't stir. Rolling up her pant leg, he inspected the damage. Nothing but a smooth calf covered in soot and deep red marks. He couldn't be sure if it was broken. The head injury was a priority.

He brushed back her long blond hair from her

face. Furrows of skin, some light, some dark, covered her neck and his heart ached for her. Once he'd scorched his finger on a cast iron skillet; it had blistered and burned for days.

But he'd never been engulfed in flames, fighting for his life or the life of his loved one. Vera's love ran deep and loyal. He'd already known that personally. She'd never passed up giving aid to anyone. The woman kept hygiene kits in her car in case she encountered a homeless person and she never ignored an elderly woman attempting to put groceries in a trunk. Vera was and had always been selfless. It was why she'd come today.

To serve. To bring justice. To stop a killer.

Mercy, he admired her. He did not admire the dip in his gut thinking about her. "Vera," he breathed. Sirens pierced through his thoughts, growing louder until the lights from the ambulance blinded him. Keegan had said the stable was unpredictable. To get in and out. He was right.

Vera stirred and a slight moan escaped her lips before she coughed and sputtered. "He ran...he ran that way..." she murmured.

He? Who? "Vera, wake up. You're dreaming."

"I'm not dreaming. If I were dreaming," she said through a groan, "I'd be on a horse by a creek or something. Maybe even eating a cheeseburger and fries without gaining weight. That's a dream, Brookie."

Her humor and even the old pet name she'd given him brought a smirk to his lips. Granted, he detested the name, but he'd always allowed her to use it. Because at one time, he'd loved her more than anything or anyone in the world.

She shifted and winced. Her frame was petite, barely over five feet. When he'd embraced her, she'd been swallowed up by his beefy six-foot-three-inch frame. But she was tough and solid. Full of spunk, even now in her wounded state. She was far from fragile.

At least physically.

Brooks now understood the brokenness of loss. The way grief shattered one's soul until even breathing hurt. Many nights after CeCe died, he'd prayed God would take him too. It would have been so much easier than the excruciating heartbreak. But then he'd retract the prayer for Katie's sake. For her, he'd had to go on and not be consumed by the pain eating him alive.

"Help me sit up."

"Your leg might be broken or you could have internal injuries. Let's wait on the paramedics."

"It's not broken or I'd have probably puked from the pain by now."

"Nice."

Vera shifted and held her head; Brooks helped her into a sitting position. She winced at her leg. "Not broken but probably sprained. My head hurts though. Not gonna lie."

The paramedics entered the stable, assessed her condition and then lifted her onto a stretcher against her wishes. "You'll need X-rays on that leg and butterfly stitches on your head." They asked several probing questions before loading her into the ambulance.

"I'll be right behind you," Brooks told her.

"Get the police out here to comb the area. I saw someone. The beam falling was deliberate." Her voice shook and her hand trembled.

"Are you sure?" She had hit her head.

"I'm positive."

"Okay." The doors closed, and Brooks massaged the nape of his neck. Why would the killer be out here? Had he returned to his other crime scenes?

But why try to hurt or kill Vera? She might have interrupted him or he was afraid she would have seen him. Or he might have left something behind and was scared she would find it first and take it. Something incriminating. Striding back into the stable, Brooks inspected the ceiling where the beam had fallen from. He kicked the actual beam. If Vera hadn't been fast on her feet, she might not be alive right now.

Brooks couldn't have another death on his hands. He already carried the guilt from Ce-Ce's death.

"Brooks, my tires are looking bald."

"I'll handle it, babe."

He'd thought he'd had time.

Time slipped by. Reminders fell on deaf ears.

And then her tire blew.

Time ended.

He'd never forgive himself for that. Never forgive himself for robbing Katie of her mom. The loss was taking serious effect. Since she'd passed, the kid was always in trouble. CeCe had been so good with her. Brooks hadn't been raised with sisters. Dealing with the female persuasion was foreign to him. He was utterly clueless when it came to their thought processes and emotions.

Tracey had been a godsend since CeCe's death. Picking up the slack and doing girl things with Katie. Now some sick dude with an affinity for fire had seemingly fixated on Tracey.

He jogged to his unmarked Dodge Charger and paused as a sudden cold swept over him and the feeling of unseen eyes staring from beyond sent a rush of dread into his blood.

This killer was unpredictable, an opportunist, and clearly not done with his agenda—one that Brooks was also clueless about. That was why he needed Vera. She could get into the killer's mind and figure out his motive and what kind of person they needed to be pursuing. She was good at reading people. She'd always been able to read him.

But then his feelings about her had always been easy to observe; he'd never held back from her. Never felt the need to. He wasn't always good with sharing his emotions but she'd made it simple for him. He wished it was as simple with Katie.

Right now, he was hanging on by a thread, being pulled in so many personal and professional directions. Thankfully, he had some help in the department now, since they'd promoted Andy Michaels from narcotics to homicide detective. The precinct was small and everyone knew everyone. Andy was a good guy and CeCe had set him up with Tracey about three months before she'd died. They had just recently gotten engaged. A wedding was set for summer. CeCe would be proud.

But even with him and Andy working the case, it was a demanding job. Busy. Stressful. Time consuming.

Everyone was looking to him for answers.

Brooks had none.

He eased onto the highway flanked by the gorgeous Davis Mountains. The winding curves he'd been driving since he was sixteen. As he approached the downtown area, he slowed. Most of Serenity Canyon's shops, boutiques and businesses had closed for the evening. Only a few restaurants and cafés were still open. Once he passed through downtown, he made his way to the small hospital with an even smaller emergency department. Parking behind the ambulance, he left his light bar flashing and headed inside.

As the doors automatically slid open, a wave of warm air enveloped him. He slumped in a waiting room chair and mindlessly scrolled through his phone. The doors opened again and he glanced up.

Andy and Tracey entered. Her expression was worried. She was supposed to be watching Katie.

"Where's Katie?" he asked.

"I dropped her at Allyson Beaumont's house fifteen minutes ago. Carinne said she can stay the night if you're going to be later than ten."

Tracey helped Brooks so much with Katie, but she had to be to bed early and at the news station by 4:00 a.m. for field reporting, so when she wasn't available, Allyson's mom, Carinne, pitched in. "I'll text her. I have no clue how long I'll be."

"Any word on your FBI friend? Andy told me she'd been attacked at the stable. That it wasn't an accident."

Andy's neck reddened. Tracey often had insider scoops and it wasn't from Brooks. He knew how to separate personal and professional lines.

"Do not report that, Tracey. We don't know enough about what happened, and I'm not one hundred percent sure that she saw anything. She hit her head pretty good." He stood and paced the waiting area.

"I'm sure she'll be fine," Tracey said. "From what you said about her in the press conference this morning, she seems fully capable and well equipped to handle these kinds of circumstances."

"Yeah, well, you didn't see her. If anything happens it'll be…"

His words died on his lips as Vera hobbled into the waiting room, papers in her right hand. Butterfly stitches and a scowl lined her brow. He rushed to her, inspecting her. "Are you okay or checking yourself out against doctors' wishes?" The woman was stubborn. Doubtful that had changed over the years.

A smirk creased the dimple in her left cheek that was streaked with soot and dirt. "No. I'm released. Headache but no concussion. Ankle's bruised, so I get to wear this beauty." She drew her left pant leg up to reveal a lightweight brace. "Better than a boot or cast, I guess. Otherwise I'm dandy."

He silently thanked God and his shoulders relaxed. "You said you saw someone. You still sure?"

"Yep."

"I believe you." He scoped out her forehead, instinctively touched the tender area. "Looks painful. I'm sorry, Vera. I feel responsible."

"You knock a beam loose and onto me? I mean you had left the scene. You had time to circle around the stable…"

He gaped then caught the twinkle in her pale green eyes, the tease twitching at the side of her lip, cocking it into a rather attractive smirk.

"Ha. Ha."

"Then don't feel sorry or responsible. I can't say it was the arsonist. It might be someone who has a fire fetish but hasn't gotten up the nerve to set his own yet, so he came out to live vicariously. I spooked him and he knocked the beam loose and ran. I don't know for sure. But I plan to find out. After I wash away all this grime. I'd like to get started tonight."

"You should rest, but before you protest, let me add I know you won't. So come meet my partner and Tracey Tisdale. Katie's at a friend's house but you can meet her tomorrow. You'll like her. Y'all share the spunky vibe." He pulled out his cell phone. "I'll text you my address. We can go to my place and go over more case information, have decent coffee. I'll drop you at the station for your rental or I can take you to the hotel and wait on you if you don't feel like driving."

She waved him off with the hand holding her papers. "I can drive. And I'd like to meet your daughter. I hope she's more like her mother. Two of you is too many." She winked and he grinned, then guided her with his hand on her lower back toward Andy and Tracey.

"She's just like her mom. But maybe a little like her old man too." He introduced her to Andy Michaels and they shook hands. "And this is Tracey Tisdale. The reporter who's received the calls, and CeCe's best friend." He turned and held Vera's gaze. "And this is my…"

Old friend? The person he once thought was the love of his life?

"Dear friend and the woman who is going to help us catch this sicko. Vera Gilmore."

Tracey grinned and hugged her. "So you're the star he talked about in the press conference earlier this morning."

Brooks hadn't used the word "star," but she was. Earlier today he'd given a press conference to help put the public at ease. Releasing the news that a behavioral expert from the FBI was coming on board as a consultant—one he had said he trusted implicitly—would help put some fear to bed. He might have added a few more accolades, but they were all true. Not a single biased statement.

"I'm glad to have you here," Tracey said. "It's been unnerving at best. Terrifying to say the least. Sooner we catch him, the sooner I can stop jumping at shadows."

"I'll do everything I can. Once I clean up."

They strode outside to the parking lot.

Andy hung back and gave Brooks a knowing grin. "A dear friend, huh?" he murmured. "I suspect something more than that, Brooks."

"That's why you're a detective. You got good gut feelings."

Andy punched his biceps. "Knew it. Told Tracey I was sure y'all knew each other in a more personal way."

"College. Thought I was gonna marry her. Even ring shopped. But…it went another way. No regrets."

"Wow. That's more personal than I suspected. Speaking of suspecting, I also think this guy is ramping up. I don't like that Tracey is in the center or that he has her personal cell number or that we can't figure out how he got it."

Brooks didn't like any of it either and Tracey wouldn't change her number.

"I think your gut is spot-on there too."

That meant they needed to be on their A games.

TWO

The Serenity Motel, nestled at the base of the Davis Mountains on the edge of Serenity Canyon, had just thirty-two rooms that could only be accessed from outside. Vera didn't mind that the room hadn't had a décor update since the early nineties. All she cared about was that it was clean and tidy and the water was hot. After freshening up and swallowing down a few over-the-counter pain relievers, she stared into the mirror. She'd reapplied her makeup. What a total heel. It was late. She had no one to impress.

"You're an idiot, Vera Bree Gilmore," she whispered. She'd brushed her long, thick hair that drove her crazy. Before the fire, she'd worn it above the shoulders, but now the longer length helped conceal scars and avoid stares and questions. Questions she didn't mind too much other than the pain they evoked at the memories of Danny's death. But what hurt most were the gawks at her hand or her neck if it happened to be exposed, then the rush to break eye contact when she caught a person looking. As if she were some kind of sideshow freak.

Vera read and pinned scriptures about beauty being fleeting but a woman who loved the Lord was to be praised. The one about women being attractive by their good works. Reading the verses reminded her daily she was far more than her outer appearance, but it was a constant battle and some days, feeling unattractive, unlovable won. Especially on days when well-meaning friends and family members told her, "Your face is still pretty."

She sighed and ignored the burn behind her eyes.

And here she was contouring and accenting to make up for the fact that everything else about her wasn't pretty. It was silly. She wasn't here to catch Brooks's eye. She was here to help catch a killer. But she couldn't bring herself to use the makeup remover wipes.

After dressing in a hoodie and yoga pants, she carefully slid into her running shoes. The brace was thin and didn't feel too tight, thankfully. She grabbed her purse from the small table by the door and headed out for Brooks's place. He'd told her he lived on a modest ranch near the river that ran through Serenity Canyon.

Shivering as she stepped into the crisp night

air, she brushed a tendril of hair back and headed for the car, favoring her uninjured foot.

An icy streak inched down her back and her chest tightened. Eyes not quite adjusted to the dark, she blinked and scanned the sparse lot. Three cars. One light glowing a few doors down. Across the street, a small grocery store had closed for the evening. But her gut warned that she wasn't alone in the parking lot.

Pressing her fob with her thumb, she quickened her pace, as best she could with the stupid bruised foot, toward her rental car. Two staccato beeps signaled her vehicle was now unlocked.

Almost there.

As she opened the driver's-side door, a hulking figure burst from the shadows and shoved her against the car; her cheekbone struck the side and bounced off. Pain sprang into her head, but her training kicked into gear. Despite the fear sending a jolt of panic into her lungs, she forced calm movements.

She slammed her elbow backward, aiming at her attacker. He grunted and hissed, "You're not going to ruin this. This is your second and final warning."

Shoving the side of her face against the cold metal of the car, he kept her arms pinned behind her back as his face pressed into the back of her head, his breath hot on her neck.

The ankle injury threw her sturdy balance off and she struggled to keep solid footing.

"If you don't leave, you'll regret it." His voice was low and raspy and his breath smelled of booze and cigarettes.

Suddenly he released her and she turned to see her assailant sprinting across the lot in a dark hoodie and jeans. She grabbed her gun from her purse to pursue him, but the pressure on her ankle sent a burst of white-hot pain through her foot. She huffed and kicked at the pavement with her good foot. Now he would get away.

Sweat dotted her forehead and her pulse galloped wildly as reality sank in. He could have killed her. But he hadn't. That meant he was intelligent enough to know killing a law enforcement officer would put a big wrench in his plan—whatever that was. Earlier, had the beam in the stable ended her life, it would be assumed an accident. Even Keegan Lane said it might not be secure for long.

But now…now there was no doubt she'd been assaulted and threatened.

While it incited fear, it also heated her blood. No one was going to tell her to back off so he could freely continue his murderous rampage.

Vera had been through the fire. Literally. She didn't quit. Didn't back down.

But she was going to be more cautious.

She climbed inside her car, locked the door and hit the navigation app. Brooks wasn't going to be thrilled when she told him about the attack.

About fifteen minutes later, she turned down a long stretch of gravel that led up to the Double B Ranch. Brooks had always been a cowboy and she loved that about him. Riding horses on his family's property had been a highlight of her trips to Serenity Canyon. She'd dreamed of living on a ranch with him, having horses. Some kids.

He was living half their dream.

As she approached the modest white ranch house, she grinned. She could totally see him making a life here. Enjoying the quiet seclusion with the mountains as a glorious backdrop. She parked behind his unmarked Charger, a blue Honda and a gray Ford truck then hobbled to the porch.

A large porch swing that looked like a twin bed full of colorful pillows rocked in the breeze. She rang the doorbell, smoothing her hair. The jitters from her altercation had ebbed on the drive over, but now she had new ones to contend with that had nothing to do with her assault and everything to do with the man at the door.

Brooks stood barefoot in a Texas A&M

sweatshirt and gray sweats. "You're later than I expected. I made coffee. Decaf. I'm getting old." The humor in his eyes died and he touched the fresh bruise on her cheek. "What happened?"

"I had a little run-in with our arsonist."

"What?" His deep voice boomed and he ushered her inside the house. The smell of coffee and vanilla filled the air. "Are you okay?"

"I am. Just a little shaken up. I'd have chased him down but..." She pointed at her ankle.

Tracey entered the foyer, concern on her face and a mug in hand. "What's going on?" She had the reporter nose and had already sniffed out a story.

Vera heaved a sigh and briefed them, including the attacker's menacing threats to her. "I'd say he was about six feet. White. He had a beard, felt it on my cheek, but I never saw anything but his hands, looked like younger hands. He didn't touch my car, so there won't be prints."

"Come on. I'll make you chamomile tea to calm you." Tracey put a lithe arm around Vera and led her into the updated kitchen. Black-and-white tiled flooring, white countertops and black cabinets. Vera sat at the rectangular kitchen table, a wall of windows revealing a rolling pasture. What a gorgeous view this would be at sunrise and sunset.

Tracey filled a kettle with water while Brooks leaned against the wall by the trash can, his arms folded over his barrel chest—apparently he still loved the gym—and his intense eyes squinted. "I want to know what this plan is."

"Join the club, Brookie."

Tracey arched an eyebrow. "Brookie?"

"I hate it." He grinned. "Old habits die hard though, huh, Veral?"

Vera chuckled. "Veral" was his pet name, referring to feral since her temper had run hot when she was younger. Her forties had mellowed her—sort of. "I guess so."

"Why would the arsonist attack you? That's weird, right?" Tracey asked.

"If I had to make an educated guess, I'd say he saw the press release and wasn't pleased at Brooks's stellar description of me—thank you, by the way. He may have been keeping tabs on Brooks and followed him to the stable earlier or he was out there for other twisted reasons. Either way, it was a chance to stop me before I got started. I survived, so he took another approach."

"Any idea who we're looking for?" Brooks asked.

"Now that I've been attacked and heard his voice, I'm officially going with a white male under forty who drinks and smokes. I smelled it on his breath when I was attacked. He probably has priors with arson, but unlikely any coupled with homicide. These are his first string. Won't be his last. He can't help himself when it comes to fire, so he's inserted himself into the crowds to watch. I'll need to get photos and go through each one carefully, see whose face shows up in each of them."

"I'll make it happen," Brooks said.

"I'm a kink in his plan," Vera said. "And he does have one. These aren't random or spontaneous crimes. He's calculated and organized, but simple. Does just enough to accomplish his goal. If I don't leave—and I'm not—he will try again to remove me from his diabolical equation."

Brooks grimaced. "And it's my fault."

"No. It's his. And after that stunt, I'm even more determined to burn down his plot. Pun intended." The kettle whistled and Tracey brought Vera a white mug full of chamomile tea. "Sugar and honey are on the table." She eased her trim figure into the chair across from her. She was camera perfect. Shiny blond hair, alert blue eyes with long lashes, and flawless skin. Vera remembered the days of smooth skin. Tracey would certainly capture the attention of someone watching the news, and had captured their killer's attention.

"Brooks said you wanted to talk to me about the case," Tracey said. "I don't have a lot of time. I have to get to bed. I need to be at work by 4:00 a.m. Can't be having circles under my eyes."

If that was Vera's greatest concern, she'd take it. "These murders happened in the early hours?"

"Yes. My first call was about four thirty, second was four and same for this last one. He knows my shift." She rubbed the inside of her thumb with her index finger. "I thought it was a joke—the first time. He said, 'There's a fire out at Twisted Shoe. He's burning alive. Go get the story. I want you to have it.' Then the line went dead. I laughed it off, but my cameraman, Ryan Peterson, said we ought to go check it out. It could be something and, if it was, we might be able to help the victim. So…we did." She placed a hand to the hollow of her throat. "It was awful. And we couldn't help him. The truck was covered in flames and smoke was so heavy, so thick…"

"But you did report it."

"Yeah," she murmured.

Because it was news. And like most reporters, they couldn't help themselves. "Twisted Shoe is in Big Bend National Park?"

"It's, uh, along the Juniper Canyon road. Real remote. One vehicle. No trailers or campers—"

"The victim had been using his truck as a camper."

Tracey nodded.

Vera turned to Brooks. "What do we know about this first victim?" In the six months since his murder, surely they had something.

He poured a cup of decaf, sipped it black. "Lonnie Kildare. Forty-three, from Lubbock. Divorced. Ex had no idea he was in Big Bend or why he would even be there. He owned a landscaping business, which his brother said was going under, but Lonnie had a plan to get it back on its feet. We looked at his financials. The company was in trouble and Lonnie had a lot of debts, including months of neglect on his child support. He has a fourteen-and twelve-year-old."

Vera sipped her tea and tapped a fingernail on the worn kitchen table. "And you didn't know him?" she asked Tracey.

"No." She shook her head. "I've never even been to Lubbock. I'm from Dallas."

"Oh, I'm a Fort Worth girl." Commonality between them.

"Nice." Her smile faltered. "But I did sort of know the second victim. Wendy Siller. An intern at the news station. She'd only been there a few weeks, but was fitting right in and had been allowed to do a couple of nighttime stories—she was good. I thought I'd end up mentoring her, not…reporting her murder." She shuddered and laid her head in her hands. "I only got an address with that phone call," she explained, looking up. "Ryan was with me. I put it on speaker. He said, 'You're better than her. Go report it.' Then he gave the address. I didn't know who *her* was. This time we immediately called the police before arriving on the scene. We knew it wasn't a joke."

"I told her to go ahead and report the news," Brooks interjected. "This guy has a fixation on his handiwork and he's chosen Tracey to air it. Or he's fixated with her and wants her to have as much fame as he does. Might see them as a pair. Regardless, I was afraid if she didn't report it, we might have another body on our hands even sooner. He killed so she could be on the news reporting it and the world could see the mess he made."

Vera sipped again, listening and allowing the information to percolate in her mind before jumping to theories. "This one was three months after the first murder?"

"Almost three. Yes," Brooks said.

Before Vera could say anything else, a car door slamming then the front door following the same action startled her.

"Why did I have to come home?" A shrill, demanding voice projected into the kitchen and Brooks groaned.

Katie.

He pushed off the wall and strode to the living room where his middle-schooler had made her grand entrance, irritated that she had to be home in her own bed on a school night. Granted, over the past two years, he'd made a heap of allowances, letting her stay over at Allyson's. But it was time to get back on track. Get on a routine. Be home more. Including himself.

"Because you live here and I said so." The ole "I said so." Something he promised he'd never to do his own kids before he'd had a kid. When Katie turned eight, it had become his new favorite phrase. Impetuous, curious, and a future leader of America, aka bossy as all get-out, Katie had stolen his heart from her first breath. But she exhausted the daylights out of him and drove him to high blood pressure and sometimes the very brink of insanity. On other days, just straight-up confusion.

"Yeah, well, whatever."

"Do not take that tone with me, young lady."

She caught his "I'm not playing around" glare and her shoulders drooped. "Yessir," she said sullenly and laid her bow and arrow against the wall. Since reading *The Hunger Games* series, she'd been obsessed with archery and had begged for lessons. She and Allyson had them on Saturday mornings and he'd set up some targets out back, hoping it would help her relieve some anger. He wasn't sure it was working but her aim was getting spot-on. "Who's parked behind Miss Tracey?"

"An old friend consulting on a case. She's an FBI agent. A profiler."

Katie's eyes lit up. Didn't matter how many times he told her to turn off *CSI* and *Criminal Minds*, she watched them anyway, along with all the cold case and true crime shows. She was a little armchair detective and secretly he was pretty proud of her. She was clever. Too clever. But too much of that darkness wasn't good for anyone.

"Whoa! That's awesome."

"Yeah." Before he could get another word in edgewise, she'd bolted into the kitchen.

"Hey, Miss Tracey."

"Hey, hon."

Brooks entered the kitchen. Katie's boisterousness had turned shy and her hands were behind her back. "Hello," she said faintly.

"Hello," Vera said with a welcoming smile. "You must be Katie. I'm Vera Gilmore."

"*Miss* Vera," Brooks corrected. He could care less about the generation or that Allyson was originally from up north and never had to say ma'am or sir. Respect was respect in his old Texan opinion. Yes, ma'am. No, ma'am. *Miss* Vera.

Vera arched a blond eyebrow and he caught her utter amusement.

"Can I call you Special Agent Gilmore?"

Vera batted her head from side to side, weighing the idea. "It's a bit formal but…" She glanced at Brooks, awaiting permission.

"Whatever," he said as he pawed his face. This wasn't a battle he was going to bear arms against.

"Cool. You hear about the fires? Someone wants to kill Miss Tracey."

Tracey sputtered over her sip of tea. "I don't think I'd go that far."

Vera leaned forward, ignoring Tracey. "Really? Why do you think that?"

Katie brightened. "You—a real life *Criminal Minds* profiler—want my opinion?"

Vera pursed her lips, holding in a laugh. Brooks sighed, but said nothing. He was curious. Katie hadn't ever voiced that opinion to him. He wasn't sure what was more disconcerting—that she speculated over the case or that she didn't seem too worried about Tracey's safety, considering she was sitting within earshot. She was more enamored with Vera. That, he could understand.

"I most certainly do," Vera said.

"I'm no professional, of course," Katie began proudly, "but the way I see it, this guy is fixated on her. I think when she's reporting the news, he thinks she's talking directly to him. Like their own special way of communicating. If he gets her more stories, then she talks to him more. It's kinda sick, though, huh?" She turned to Tracey, who sat wide-eyed. "No offense, Miss Tracey. But everyone knows that stalkers end up trying to kill their obsession."

Brooks wasn't sure if his kid needed additional therapy or a job on the force. "You read entirely too much true crime and watch way too many crime shows. Get ready for bed."

"But it's a solid profile, isn't it?" Katie asked.

Vera tossed Brooks an apologetic expression then focused on Katie. "It's rather insightful and extremely possible. I'd wondered that myself earlier."

"For real?"

"For real."

"Hey, I gotta get ready for bed." She pointed to Brooks with her thumb. "The old man says I need some shut-eye, but you wanna see my true crime book collection? I get most of them from this used bookstore downtown. Do you know how many bodies John Wayne Gacy had in his crawl space?"

Vera blinked in succession and her mouth

hung slightly open. "I do actually, and I'd love to see your book collection."

"Bed," Brooks said sternly. "Miss Vera, or Agent Gilmore, whatever, can see them tomorrow."

Katie groaned. "Yessir." She made a dramatic display of exiting and Brooks sighed and slumped in a chair next to Vera.

"So that's my kid."

Vera laughed. "She's bright and colorful."

"And a challenge," Tracey offered and stood. "I have to get some shut-eye too, but quite frankly, after that conversation I don't want to go home. Maybe I can get Andy to do some drive-bys tonight if nothing big is going down at the precinct."

Brooks wasn't surprised the dark conversation would affect Tracey. When the first murder happened and then the second, Tracey had expressed her fear and wanted to run and hide. But Brooks explained the importance of her continuing to report the news and not anger the killer. He had to know more. What if he was wrong? What if the killer did plan to abduct and murder her like Katie and Vera suspected?

"Do you think he wants to kill me, Brooks?"

Brooks couldn't lie. "The truth is I have no idea what game he's playing. Why don't you and Vera both stay here? Andy's working and can't be driving by your house all night. And after the attack at the hotel, Vera, I'd feel better if you stayed here where I can have your back. We have plenty of room."

Vera shifted uncomfortably in her chair. "Oh, I don't know, Brooks."

"I have a guest room downstairs and one upstairs. Both have private baths. Plus I have state-of-the-art security, at least when Katie isn't disarming it and— Never mind."

Four times she'd sneaked out of the house since CeCe had passed. Three times he'd found her on the south end of the property where a small chapel had been built for cattle ranchers in the 1920s. It had been what CeCe called her War Room. A place she went to pray and do spiritual warfare on behalf of her family. She'd been the pillar of this family and Katie had gone to be close to her and to pray. The other time she'd been angry at Brooks for grounding her and she'd run away. She'd made it a mile down the road before Tracey called saying Katie was on her way to her house.

"I'd sleep better knowing you both are here," Brooks added.

Tracey sighed. "I need to gather up some stuff. I have nothing with me and I have to be at work. I'll call Andy to escort me."

"Good." He turned to Vera.

"Okay, but I prefer the downstairs guest room." She cleared her throat. "I keep a small bag in the car—even rentals—in case of overnight stuff. I'm good until morning."

His heart relaxed. "I'll show you to your room." He escorted her through the living room, but she moved slow, inspecting everything. He'd left all of CeCe's feminine touches from throw pillows and decorative blankets to the candles and picture frames on the mantel. Vera paused at the family photos. She touched one of him and CeCe.

"She was beautiful." Vera gazed into Brooks's eyes. "They say the first year is the hardest, but they all feel hard to me."

He nodded. "Yeah," he said through a clogged gullet. "We're making it. Barely. Katie's…she's having a hard time, and it's coming out in negative behavior. Now that her soccer coach is dead, I fear what she'll do. Some days she's the kid she was before CeCe passed—like tonight. Her excitement over you. The obsession with true crime has always been there. She's a puzzle solver and always sticks up for the underdog—I can see the justice seeker in her. But some days it's like the grief swallows her and she gets angry—which I know is a stage. Been through it recently myself."

"She in counseling?"

"Yes. At our church."

"Good. She needs it, and she needs you. She'll get through it."

"I hope so. I try to be here, but you know the job. Not that we see a lot of homicide in Serenity Canyon, but that's not all I do. Lately, I've been dealing with this. I'm trying to be everything she needs, Vera. But I'm coming up short."

"Brooks, you can't be *everything* to her. To anyone. Be her father. That's what she needs from you. Be present when you are with her. God will see you through the rest. He's seen me through, though I admit I still have hard days. Days that…well, just hard days."

She didn't want to get deep into it. He understood. It had been a long day and they were both exhausted. And some things about grief were private. "Let me show you to your room. It's right next to mine." They passed Katie's room and he heard her stirring, saw the light glow from underneath the door. "Katie Bug," Brooks said through the door, "it's lights out."

"Yessir."

The lamplight went out.

"Love you."

"Love you too."

Down the hall, he opened the door and switched on the lamp. "Fresh towels and stuff are under the sink. If you need anything, let me know."

Vera nodded and strode to the window, peeking out. "I like your place."

"Thanks. When Mom passed, I used the insurance money to put down on it. I'll show you around tomorrow. Get some—" His attention flashed on movement outside.

Vera's spine straightened and her eyes widened. "What is it?" She turned back toward the window.

"Someone's out there."

THREE

Vera's breath caught in her throat. Had the man from the motel followed her here? Was he keeping tabs on her to see if she'd obey his orders and leave town? Well, she wasn't. But the fear that opened up into flight mode screamed for her to run.

Under the thumbnail of moonlight, she caught sight of a looming figure skulking outside, moving slowly, methodically. It was almost 10:00 p.m. "Tracey hasn't left yet," Vera whispered. She had no business leaving the house now.

Brooks kicked into gear. "Keep an eye out. I'll tell her to stay put. Then I'm going out there."

"I'll back you up," she said, already having drawn her weapon.

Brooks glanced at her foot.

"Half a back is better than no back," she insisted. Besides, if she had to push past the pain to get a job done, she could. She had the scars to prove it. She'd dragged Danny down the flight of stairs—well, they'd fallen most of the way since he'd been unconscious—into the living room and out the front door, but the smoke inhalation had done too much damage.

"Good point."

He rushed from the room and she heard voices outside in the hallway. The figure moved from her line of sight and she hurried into the hallway. "He's moving behind the house."

"Tracey," Brooks said, "lock yourself in Katie's room. Make up a reason to be in there. I don't want to frighten her."

Tracey nodded, her crystal-blue eyes wide with fear, and she tapped on Katie's door. "Hey, Katie Bug. Can I come in?"

"Yes, ma'am."

She slipped inside then Brooks blew toward the kitchen, which gave him a view of the backyard. "You ready?"

"I got you." Vera licked her lips, let the adrenaline fuel her fight mode, and kept her hands steady on her gun. Her finger rested by the trigger but not on it, her Maglite in the other hand.

Brooks opened the kitchen door and they slipped into the night. The temperature had dropped to the cool fifties but it felt good on Vera's flushed skin.

Inching along the back of the house, they kept to the shadows, pausing every few beats to listen. A rustling twenty feet out drew their attention. Footsteps along grass came closer.

"Freeze," Brooks bellowed with that rumbly deep voice. No longer like butter but menacing and authoritative.

"Whoa, big fella," a male voice returned. She recognized it but couldn't place it.

"Andy?" Brooks shone his light in the direction, and Andy Michaels raised his hands to shield his eyes.

Wearing jeans and a dark dress shirt, he frowned. "What's going on? Tracey texted she was heading home to pack a bag and wanted me to follow her. When I got here, I saw someone skulking around the house."

So they had seen someone. Not Andy.

"Why didn't you call or text?" Brooks lowered his light. "I could have killed you. She could have killed you." He pointed his thumb at Vera.

"Instinct. Sorry, dude. Anyway, I lost him." Andy approached and holstered his weapon. "Tracey said you think this guy is going to kill her if he can't have her. True?" he asked as they strode to the house and entered the kitchen.

Vera rubbed her lower back. The day had been long. She was beat up, sore, and her eyes were dry and itchy. But Andy had a right to know what he was dealing with when it came to his fiancée.

"I think he's fixated on her," Vera said. "He's now choosing people connected to her. Not sure why. We need more information. We'll search and see if any other reporters have been stalked or sent letters. Had Tracey received letters prior to the first phone call and fire?"

"No," Andy said. "I asked. But I'll run down other reporters, find out about them. I texted Tracey the coast is clear."

Brooks nodded. "Check reporters being stalked in neighboring cities. He may have recently moved here."

Tracey rushed into the kitchen, her phone in hand, and she fell into Andy's arms. "Why were you out there alone?"

"It's okay, baby." He caressed her head. "You're safe now. I won't let anyone hurt you."

"How's Katie?" Brooks asked.

"She thought I was sneaking in to chat about the profiler." Tracey grinned. "She's asleep now."

Brooks nodded. "Good. We need to make sure to keep the alarm set."

"Maybe I should go back to the motel. I don't want to endanger Katie, Brooks." The last thing Vera wanted was to put a child in danger.

"Me too. Back to my apartment, that is,"

Tracey agreed. "We can't be sure which one of us he was here for." Tracey grabbed Vera's hand and squeezed. Vera returned it.

"No one is going anywhere. We agreed that Tracey still needs to work her shift. If she gets another call, one of us will be there. He's never told her to not call the cops. I can't keep eyes on that many places. I'd appreciate everyone under one roof. The security system here is good."

Vera didn't want to put anyone out or at risk and she liked to do yoga in the morning in a tank top, comfy boxer shorts and with her hair up. Well, she could do it locked in her room. There was no point arguing with Brooks. The man was stubborn and always had been. "Fine. Let me get my bag."

"I'll come along," Brooks said. It wasn't up for debate. Stepping onto the porch, Vera waited a beat and listened. Rustling from the horses in the stable carried along the crisp air.

"You can see stars for miles out here," Vera murmured.

"That, you can." Brooks kept his gun in hand and eased off the porch steps, steady and brisk. The walkway led out to the small circle drive, where a modest three-tier fountain bubbled and gurgled. "You know, the circumstances sure stink but…" He paused and held her gaze. "I'm glad you're here. To see you again. It's weird.

In a way it's like I'm just meeting you and in another it's like we never broke up and moved on with our lives."

Vera's pulsed kicked up a notch. "You've made a great life here. Katie is fabulous. Maybe one day she'll run the BAU. She definitely has insight—remarkable for someone so young. But I guess kids grow up faster nowadays. Wow, I sound old."

He laughed. "I feel old most days."

"You look great." Heat bloomed in her cheeks and her stomach swirled. Why did she have to go and say that? Why did he have to say it was like they'd never broken up?

"So do you."

Lies. She laughed. "Sure."

"What? You do. I don't think you've aged."

"Good makeup and an even better hair stylist. I pay to be blonder than I am." She snorted and he grinned. She pressed the fob and the trunk unlocked. Brooks raised it and hauled out her emergency duffel bag.

"You always were the most organized woman I know. You still highlight information in different colors based on subject matter?"

"Well, of course." She locked the car when he closed the trunk.

Brooks paused on the porch. "Hey, when I introduced you today as an old friend…it's not because I was trying to hide our past, but I don't want them to think I'm biased because we used to love each other."

Those words withered her lungs, stole her breath.

They had loved each other.

After the breakup, she'd second-guessed the decision, her choice to enter the FBI academy, and resigned herself to never fall in love again. But she'd chosen her first dream.

And then she'd met Danny. Polar opposite of Brooks with a few similarities. Their love had been a slow bloom, but beautiful.

"When I said you were the best in your field during the press conference, I meant it, Vera. I've followed some of your more high-profile cases. I'm proud of you and what you've become. You made the right choice."

The words of affirmation hit her in a soft spot. "Thank you. That means so much to me." She regained some composure and inwardly lost it again when he enveloped her hand in his big, warm one. Her unpuckered hand. Insecurity reared its ugly head. Why had he chosen that hand? Was touching her other one too unappealing?

"I'm going to do everything in my power to keep you safe. You can trust me."

She'd always trusted Brooks. He'd never

given her reason not to. She could and would trust him on this investigation, but as far as her heart went…well, he was holding her unscarred hand. "I do trust you." Tears welled in her eyes, surprising her and aggravating her all at once.

He brushed one away. "I hate to see you cry, Vera. Always have." He slowly drew her against him, her head resting on his breastbone. She needed to pull away. Guard her heart. But when he held her, she felt like a caterpillar in a safe cocoon. Only, she wasn't breaking free to become a beautiful butterfly. The fire had robbed her of that.

And he'd only held her good hand.

"Why are you crying?" he asked softly.

"I don't know." Because fond memories surfaced. Because she was thinking of Danny. Because she wanted to feel beautiful—to Brooks. Stress. A million other reasons.

The front door opened. Tracey and Andy stepped out, invading the intimate moment. Vera's cheeks flamed again and she stepped from the embrace and smoothed her hair, nonchalantly brushing stray tears.

"We're sorry," Andy said. "We didn't realize—"

"You're fine," Vera said. "Just old friends having a moment."

Tracey cocked her head, gave her a knowing

expression. "You were more than old friends," she said and slipped her arm through Andy's.

"We were," Brooks admitted. "Don't report that though. Vera is here because she's worth her salt professionally. Not because we...well, we almost got married."

"I need more than CliffsNotes, Brooks."

Andy put an arm around her. "He can tell it all later. We need to go." He led Tracey to the car.

Brooks and Vera watched as Andy and Tracey drove away. Vera was about to open the door when a crack thundered.

And a bullet shattered the porch light above her head.

Brooks hauled Vera into the house as another bullet slammed into one of the four porch pillars and stole his breath.

"Daddy?"

Katie. No. She was supposed to be asleep. All-encompassing fear snaked around him, suffocating.

"Katie, don't—"

The sentence died on his lips as his precious bleary-eyed and barefoot little girl stepped into the open.

Into the line of fire.

"Katie!" He hurled himself toward her.

Another shot fired.

Vera reached her first, and dove onto the entryway floor, shielding her—her own back now an open target.

Katie shrieked.

Brooks blindly returned fire into the darkness ahead, not worried about hitting anyone innocent out there in the middle of nowhere. After squeezing off one more, he slammed the door.

Vera had Katie against the wall in a seated position and her knees up to her chest. "Just like if there was a tornado drill at school."

Katie tucked her head and covered it with her arms.

"Good girl." Vera sprang up, cut the light in the living room then peeked out the large family room window before grabbing the curtain and swinging it across the rod to seal off the shooter's view inside.

Brooks called 9-1-1.

"Okay, hon. Into the hall closet." She helped Katie up, and hurried her into the closet in the hall. "Stay here until your daddy or I tell you to come out. Scooch all the way back."

"I'm scared."

"I know, hon. You'll be okay. Me and your daddy aren't going to let anything happen to you. Now, hunker down. Think like a profiler." She winked and closed the door.

Brooks ended the call and mouthed *Thank you*, but it seemed weak. Vera would have died for his flesh and blood. Could have died. A sudden urge to kiss her overtook his right mind. He shoved it away and a twinge of guilt nipped at him. The thought sort of felt like cheating on CeCe.

"SC police are on the way. It's too dark and there's too much terrain to go out there and hunt him. He could have night goggles for all we know." Brooks wasn't going to put them in harm's way if he could help it. They were safer inside the house.

She nodded once and kept to the wall, her chest rising and falling rapidly. "I guess he realized I'm sticking around and either tried to kill me or he wanted me to know he meant business."

No more shots had been fired since they'd closed the door and switched off the lights. "Katie Bug, you okay?"

"Yessir," his daughter's shaky voice called from inside the closet.

"Be brave, baby girl. As soon as the police arrive and check the grounds, I'll get you out. But you're safe in there."

"I know. I have my cell phone light on. Is that okay, Daddy?"

Daddy. It had been ages since she'd called

him that. He'd been reduced to Dad since the angry spell began after CeCe died. Hearing her tiny, unsure voice swelled in his heart, reminding him of the days when he was her entire world and could do no wrong. Lately it felt like everything he did was wrong. "Yeah, baby. It's okay."

"Is it the fire guy?"

"Maybe." Brooks couldn't be sure, but he had a hunch. Who else would be targeting them? "I'll call Andy to keep Tracey at her apartment a little while longer to be safe. Last thing we need is them returning while the killer is out there lying in wait." He whispered to keep his frightening words from his daughter's ears.

"Agreed," Vera said in a low tone.

Vera had thrown a wrench in the arsonist's plans. Enough that he was seething and willing to murder outside his MO to get the job done.

Blue lights flashed outside. Help had arrived.

Two officers stepped inside. Behind them, Keegan Lane clambered out of his white truck. "Had the radio on. Heard. Thought maybe I could help."

"Can you go out there and catch the jerk?"

"Maybe." He chuckled and showed his affection by slapping Brooks on the back. After giving statements, they searched the terrain as crime scene techs combed the area for bullets and casings.

It was going to be a long night.

Morning light peeped overhead quicker than Brooks would have liked. He was spent, and his eyes were dry and red from lack of sleep. After hauling Katie from the closet, he'd hung on and only released her when she'd whined and wiggled free, but she hadn't minded him sitting with her until she finally fell asleep. Before he'd left her room, he'd noticed her bow and arrow next to her under the covers. Poor thing shouldn't have to be so afraid she felt the need to sleep with her weapon.

This morning, he was going to allow her to take Friday off, but she'd woken up and wanted to go to school. Probably because it gave her a new true crime story to tell.

Andy and Tracey had arrived at the ranch about midnight, and she'd gone straight to bed then left with Andy's escort for the news station about three thirty, mumbling about no amount of makeup in the world fixing the circles under her eyes.

Vera had been up around the same time and brewed extra-strong coffee, like the kind a spoon would stand up in. He could have hugged her. But after that fleeting thought of kissing her last night, he'd pulled his thoughts together.

Now, they were almost to Twisted Shoe where the first victim, Lonnie Kildare, had been burned in his truck-turned-camper.

The sun hid behind a roll of clouds, leaving the temperature cool enough to wear his suit coat. Vera wore a soft gray sweater the color of the sky and a pair of black pants. Her black blazer lay on her lap and her shiny blond hair hung over her shoulders, thick and luxurious. When he'd dated her, she'd worn it shorter. Either way, she was lovely and it suited her.

"Why are you staring at me and not the road? I feel your eyes on me."

"First of all, I'm not staring. Just noticing your hair is longer is all. And I am paying attention to the road." The narrow backcountry road was paved with dirt and flanked with brush. Mountains surrounded them, dark and brown. A plume of dust trailed behind his Ford truck. He'd opted not to bring the unmarked unit since they'd be on bumpy mountain terrain.

"Think we'll see a bear?" Vera asked.

"I hope not."

"I do—from the safety of the truck that is." She chuckled as the bumpy road jostled her and she gripped the handle above the door. "Talk about rugged and remote. Why did this guy pick Twisted Shoe to camp?"

"Maybe because it's rugged and remote. Needed to do some thinking about his business. Clear his head under the stars."

"Or he was planning on meeting someone out here. You said his business was in trouble but he knew a way to fix it. What if his fix was here—not necessarily in Serenity Canyon, but a lot of towns surround Big Bend. We need to see if we can connect him to someone nearby. They might be able to help us put some pieces together. Because this doesn't make sense."

"What doesn't?" Brooks hit a hole and the truck dipped and bounced. A lot like his life recently. CeCe's death and the aftermath. Now this case. The road was narrow and dirty. One he'd never driven before. He didn't know where the divots were and he'd hit every single one only to be jostled and shaken. He longed for fresh paved roads. Smooth and stretched out along a beautiful view. But who knew if he'd ever get that life back again—if he'd ever even had that kind of road. Nothing had come easy or been easy for Brooks.

"Why would the killer pick Twisted Shoe, which is over thirty minutes from Serenity Canyon and in this remote place, to set a fire on some random guy? Why not light up a camp-site closer to town? Easier to get to."

"Privacy."

Vera chewed on the edge of her thumbnail. "Possibly. But something isn't sitting pretty with me. I want to know more about Lonnie Kildare."

About six miles later, they made it to the remote site, which was cordoned off by old wooden logs. The truck/camper had been taken into custody by CSI to comb for trace evidence. As of now, they had found nothing of significance except a glass bottle that had been discovered in the cab, but no prints. He'd told her all that, but Vera wanted to see the actual site. Get a feel.

As Vera clambered out of the truck, a gust of wind lifted her hair and blew it in her face. She swiped it away but didn't bother pulling it back. He noticed the puckered skin at the edge of the neck of her sweater. His stomach clenched as he imagined her surrounded by that raging fire, feeling trapped. No wonder she'd chosen the downstairs guest room.

"It's beautiful and creepy out here all at the same time," she said, spinning in a slow circle and surveying her surroundings. She cocked her head and he observed her shift into deep-thinking mode. "I'm Lonnie Kildare from Lubbock. Divorced. Business on the brink of going under.

I drive over four hours to the middle of nowhere to camp in the back of my truck. Why do I come out here to get some perspective on life when there are so many other places to camp— and for free?" She walked the path of the logs, studying the ground. "I'm out here for a reason. I've chosen this location for a specific purpose." She stopped. "Is Tracey sure she doesn't know Lonnie Kildare?"

"She says she doesn't."

"What if she's encountered him and doesn't recall? He bumped into her at a gas station or grocery store. Serenity Canyon would be the closest place to gather camping supplies. The killer might have seen a brief exchange between them. I realize it's a stretch, but I don't believe the killer targeted him randomly. He picked him for a purpose. Tracey has to be the connection." She rubbed her chin. "When you asked her if she knew Lonnie, was her fiancé present? Maybe she lied because she was keeping a secret from Andy."

"I've known Tracey for a long time. She's not keeping anything or anyone from Andy."

Vera sighed. "Until we know for sure, we'll keep running down the theory that the killer chose a stranger, then an acquaintance, then a casual friend. Next will be someone even more personal. But I'm still hanging on to the belief that this victim has meaning to our killer, which connects to Tracey. If only in his mind."

Brooks's head turned fuzzy. If the killer chose someone more personal to Tracey as his next victim, it could be any one of them. Andy. Brooks. Ryan. Even Katie.

"Then we have to find him first."

There was no other choice.

FOUR

Vera had a huge puzzle and some of the pieces—mainly Lonnie Kildare—weren't fitting. It was like the manufacturer had thrown in a piece from another puzzle as a joke. But this was no joke. Lives were being taken in brutal ways and Vera was stumped. Something she didn't like to admit, but it was true.

She considered calling two of her former colleagues and friends, who now resided nearby. Chelsey Banks-Holliday only lived a couple of hours away in El Paso with her Texas Ranger husband, Tack. And Duke Jericho had accepted a job a few months ago as lead detective in Gran Valle to be closer to his fiancée, Brigitte, who was a patrol officer and forensic artist in Los Artes. A spring wedding was on the calendar. Both Duke and Chelsey were excellent profilers and would have valuable wisdom.

And Vera wasn't too proud to ask.

After she finished the victimology, she might

have a better idea of the killer's mind and motive. Tracey had mentioned in her interview that the killer had chosen the news intern because he hadn't wanted Wendy Siller to get glory that belonged to Tracey. He must have seen the intern's field reporting and felt protective over Tracey, or he'd been irritated that when he'd turned on the news to see Tracey, it hadn't been her. But why Katie's soccer coach, Adrianna?

This killer was infatuated with Tracey but he appeared to want to hurt her too. The line between love and hate was a fine one for warped psyches. He may have been raised by a mother who'd been cruel and vindictive in the name of tough love, meted out discipline for his own good. That would certainly fracture a person's perception of love, making it far from tender and sacrificial. It would look selfish and feel like torture.

He was torturing Tracey now. And Vera—in a more overt manner. Not as obsession but opposition. An obstacle in carrying out his well-crafted plan.

Vera walked along the edge of the tree line, not sure what she was searching for. Brooks stayed out of her way, giving her space to work. The shrill timbre of his cell phone jerked her from her thoughts. His frown and stiff posture clued her in that the call wasn't pleasant.

"How did no one notice she was gone? Where was the teacher? She's where? She did what?" His baritone lowered by the second until it was nothing but a vibrating rumble. "I'll be there in forty minutes. I'm in Big Bend. No, don't call Tracey. She's at work. Let her sit there and think about what she did and stew in it awhile. But also, don't let her get too afraid." His tone softened. "Tell Bella Lee I said thank you. I'll personally go by and see her, along with my little thief." He sighed heavily. "Yeah. Okay." He ended the call.

"So, my kid decided to skip school, dragging her best friend Allyson with her, and they ended up on the square shoplifting from Bella Lee Monroe at Bella Lee's Boutique. She caught her and called the precinct. Didn't want to press charges, just scare her. I hope it did." He massaged the back of his neck. "I don't want to cut it short here—"

"No. No, I'm good. We can go right now. I'm sorry."

"She's a good kid, Vera. But since CeCe died, she's been caught trespassing on private property twice, stole a stop sign with two friends, which as you know is a felony. But I'm a cop and I grew up in this small town, so I get some slack, but I'm not sure how long the rope is."

They trudged to the truck and Brooks opened

the passenger door for her. Even in deep thought and turmoil, he was a gentleman. Vera wasn't one to take opening doors for women as a slap in the face. She quite appreciated it.

"She's angry. That's understandable." Vera clicked her seat belt in place. "Doesn't excuse bad behavior."

"Delinquency is the word you're looking for, I'm afraid." He gripped the wheel and the tires crunched along loose gravel as he drove down the dirt road.

"I'm not judging, so don't misunderstand, but how much time are you spending with her?" She cleared her throat, hoping not to overstep bounds. "I mean…the trouble she's getting into are things related to the law. Things that will get your personal attention. There are a myriad of ways to act out, but she's choosing to break the law. You're a lawman. And she's escalating."

Like their killer. What he was doing wasn't enough. He wanted more attention from Tracey and also to punish the victims.

Was Katie trying to punish her father? Vera would keep that to herself.

"I tried talking gently. I tried grounding her. I've never been one to spank, though my daddy would have disagreed with that." He smirked. "She knows the law. She knows how much trouble this could land her in. Bella could have pressed charges." His pressure increased on the pedal and they zoomed ahead faster. "Just because I'm a cop doesn't mean I can always make her wrongdoings go away, and quite frankly, I'm not sure I'd be doing her any favors if I did. She has to learn, but if she keeps this up..."

Vera laid a hand on his biceps. "Let's not think the worst just yet. She's only twelve." But he was right. She was a clever girl. And likely she thought that Brooks would sweep her behavior under the rug, that she wouldn't reap any consequences because her dad was the law. But good fathers didn't allow their children to go undisciplined for bad choices. Didn't mean they didn't love them. Her own father had let her stew in her consequences on many occasions and it had done her good in the end. She sure had been miffed at him during the process though.

"When I was fourteen, I sneaked out with the keys to my mama's car. Went joyriding with my best friend Tara. I lost control and went through Miss Birdie's yard. Somehow I went through two pine trees without hitting them, dodged her flower bed made from a huge tire, and the fake deer, drove right between the ditch and the wooden logs down her driveway and ended up in the ditch across the street." She laughed. "We called a friend who came with his mom and they pulled us out. But that night when Daddy drove home, he noticed tire ruts in Miss Birdie's yard and leaves and dirt all under Mama's car. He put two and two together."

Brooks chuckled. "I didn't know that story."

"Well, it's not one I tell often. I had to lay sod in Miss Birdie's yard to smooth out the tire ruts, wash her car every Saturday for two months—she didn't even drive anymore so it wasn't dirty but..." She shrugged. "And I was grounded. Man, I was so mad at Daddy. But I deserved the discipline. It fit the crime and I learned my lesson."

"Were you mad at your dad? Is that why you took the car?"

"No. I just wanted to joyride with Tara." She laughed. "My point is that it could have been much worse and you're right. You can't let it go."

"But you think she's angry at me for not spending as much time with her as she thinks I should. So she's hitting me where it counts—work."

He was perceptive. "Possibly."

"Every day off, every spare moment, I spend with her, but I have to work. I have to provide, and occasionally my cases go overtime. Not often. But I was a little distant after CeCe died. I was grieving too," he murmured. "I was present but I wasn't present. You know?"

"I do."

They continued their drive in mostly comfortable silence. Brooks needed time to ruminate on the conversation, the case.

Arriving at Serenity Canyon police station, a dark brick building with a slate-gray roof and picture windows lining the front, Brooks whipped into a parking space at the side entrance.

"You want me to wait in the truck?" she asked.

"No, you might as well come in, get a bad cup of coffee, and if it takes long, we have a conference room set up for the investigation. I have files in there."

She'd gone straight to the scene yesterday and hadn't been given the chance to study the case files properly.

She joined him inside. Behind a glassed-in reception desk, a woman with purple-rhinestone glasses perched on her nose tossed Brooks a pity grin and pointed down the hall.

"Thanks, Madge."

"I gave her a Coke and some Nabs."

"'Preciate it."

Madge eyed Vera and Brooks paused. "Sorry. This is Special Agent Vera—"

"Gilmore. I know." Madge looked the type to not miss any details whether she should be privy or not. "I'll get you a Coke and Nabs, too, if you need them."

Vera flashed her a professional but kind smile. "Thanks. I appreciate it. But right now, I just want to look at files."

"I'm here eight to five, so holler if you need anything."

The smells of cleaning solution and masculinity wafted down the small hall. She didn't see many female officers around. Not surprising. They passed the dispatch office on the left and a smattering of offices on the right then entered the bullpen. Katie shifted in a chair beside an officer's desk. Her Coke and crackers looked untouched.

Hair had fallen from her French braid and she looked even younger than twelve. Glancing up, she spotted Brooks and her eyes widened, but then she crossed her arms over her chest and hardened her gaze.

So she was going to take the rebellious front. *Bad choice, kiddo.*

Brooks towered over her for a few beats then huffed from his nose. "Why? Why would you do that, Katie?"

She refused to meet his eyes. "I don't know why I did it."

Maybe she didn't, maybe she did, but her

clipped tone wasn't going to score any points with her dad.

"We'll discuss this further at home. After we stop at Bella Lee's and you apologize and take your punishment like a woman."

"Yessir."

Katie tagged along behind Brooks, shoulders hunched and head hung. When Vera slung her arm around Katie, the girl leaned into her then looked up. "I shouldn't have gotten Allyson in trouble," she squeaked.

At least she was remorseful for that. "No, you shouldn't have." Vera slowed their pace. Brooks, either not hearing or pretending not to, strode to the truck. "You know, if you keep getting in trouble, you'll miss your shot at being a tip-top profiler. Petty theft is beneath you anyway," she said with a wink. "You disappointed your dad."

Katie wrapped her arms around her middle as they made their way to the truck. "Well, he disappointed me first."

Vera's heart sank. As she suspected, Katie was playing the tit-for-tat game. "You should tell him that, instead of getting in trouble with the law. He's a tough guy and can handle your feelings, Katie. Bottling up emotions is no good. Eventually they explode and stick to everything, making an awful mess. Believe me, I know."

"Angry criminals explode on you?"

Vera paused. "I'm talking about personal experience. I lost my husband to a fire. And I was mad at my Heavenly Father. Acting out just like you to pay Him back. To lash out. No good came from it until I got honest with Him."

Katie didn't respond, but Vera knew she'd heard her. The rest was up to Brooks and Katie. She wasn't sure why he'd disappointed or angered Katie, and it wasn't any of her business unless Katie or Brooks wanted to confide in her. It was for them to work out in private.

Just father and daughter.

Brooks's neck and shoulders ached from stress. The job. Katie. Bella Lee had shown a huge amount of grace, accepted the apology, and for the next three Saturdays, Katie was to help her unload and stock the shelves from seven until noon. Hard work would develop character. He hoped.

Katie's apology to Bella Lee appeared genuine, but the second she was in the truck with Brooks, she was back to the hardened shell. One minute she was his loving daughter who wanted to go horseback riding with him and the next she acted like he'd wrecked her world.

He had.

Quietly, he closed her bedroom door and padded into the kitchen, his bones weary and tired. Vera had made coffee and the nutty brew infused his senses with the promise of some renewed energy, but it would only last a little while. True strength required something more powerful and lasting than caffeine. He needed to be in the Word. To pray and get direction and guidance in so many areas, especially concerning Katie.

"You still take yours black?" Vera asked.

"I do." He slumped at the kitchen table, gazing out the floor-to-ceiling windows at the pasture. Wind rattled the windows as the temperature dipped and the clouds grew heavy with rain to come later this afternoon.

Vera handed him a steaming cup of coffee and he accepted it with a weak smile. "Thanks."

She sat across from him, her right leg curling up under her, the steam from her mug pluming in front of her face. Her lovely face with eyes fixed on him, concern and patience blooming bright. She said nothing, just waited. Expectantly. It was her way. She never pressured or pushed. Simply sat silent. Either was fine. Talking or not.

"She's mad at me. I know that. But not every day. So I don't get it."

"She doesn't want to be mad at you, Brookie. She loves you. She's torn. Be patient. She'll let it fly at some point. I hope earlier than later."

Brooks sipped his strong coffee. The way he liked it. "I hope so too. The next thing she steals might be my unmarked unit."

Vera snickered over her cup. "Let's pray she doesn't escalate to that."

"I pray every single day, all day. I noticed your sweet way with her. Thank you for that. She admires you." He swallowed and gently placed his mug down. "I admire you too."

Had he overstepped his bounds?

"I heard parts of your conversation when y'all weren't whispering. Just acted like I didn't. Katie seemed to need it." He shrugged one shoulder and glanced away, but he caught her soft pink cheeks. She'd warmed to his words. Good. He'd meant for them to blanket her.

"I hope I didn't overstep."

They were both tiptoeing around one another in different ways. Trying to be mindful of boundaries. After so many years, it was strange. They'd gone from friends to a couple then back to people who hadn't seen one another in ages. They were certainly colleagues, but a tight band stretched between them, one that seemed to be giving way, softening. Undefined.

"Not at all. I appreciated it. She sure didn't want to talk to me." He pushed his coffee aside, no longer able to enjoy it knowing there was a rift between him and his daughter.

Vera laid her dainty hand over his, the un-injured one. He'd noticed she used it predominantly. "She will. Girls are complex even on good days. Men rarely understand us."

"Amen," he groused. "Why can't there be some kind of manual or guide?"

"I'll get on that right after we catch this arsonist slash murderer." She winked and his stomach constricted, sending a rush of adrenaline through him and then a wave of guilt for his attraction. He pulled his hand away and she blushed, then balled her hand and tucked it under the table, suddenly interested in the scene outside the window.

It wasn't her. She had done nothing wrong. It was him. And if he tried to explain his withdrawal, he'd have to admit it was from visceral emotion concerning her. That would be inappropriate and unprofessional. So he pushed back his chair, the wooden legs scraping against the tile, and stood. "I think I'm going to take a walk. Clear my head." He needed grounding. He'd floated into places he had no business going.

"Sure. I can check on Katie and, for all your hospitality, let me cook for you. Least I can do to say thanks."

"I called you in to consult. I should be cooking for you. Besides, you've been attacked twice and threatened. You're welcome," he deadpanned.

"You know I make a mean lasagna."

So true. "In that case, *mi* kitchen *es su* kitchen. I can't rightly say I have any of the ingredients though."

"I'll run to the store when you get back. I don't feel comfortable leaving Katie alone in the house."

Neither did Brooks. "I'll tell you what. You run to the store and I'll go for that walk when you get back. I remember that sauce takes some time to simmer." He didn't feel comfortable letting Vera run to the grocery alone, but there was a fine line between being protective and cautious and overbearing and controlling. Vera was a trained agent. Smart. Savvy. Capable. He had to trust her, even if her bruised ankle had slowed her down some.

Right now it was Brooks who couldn't trust himself—at least, not his heart.

That was dangerous.

Vera returned from the corner market about two miles from the house. The family owned establishment and kindness from its staff reminded her of visiting Gran in Buffalo Gap. Small town. No strangers, only community. It tugged deep inside. Funny, all those years ago when she'd visited Serenity Canyon, the small-town life hadn't moved her like it did now in her forties. She'd been ready to get out there and make a mark on evil. Kick it in the rear as a federal agent. And she had. Her job was satisfying and of value.

Maybe it was the time on the ranch, though it hadn't been even a full forty-eight hours. Days stretched longer. Time eked by and yet, with a killer in their midst, it was also a whirlwind. Maybe it was the short time spent with Katie, the maternal instincts kicking in and the biological clock ticking. She and Danny had put off having children for their careers, believing they'd had plenty of time.

Brooks opened the front door and released her from the burden of heavy grocery sacks. Relief filled his eyes. Yes, she was safe. Nothing weird had happened at the tiny market. It had been a little cocoon from the mayhem. She'd enjoyed purchasing fresh mozzarella, plump tomatoes for her homemade sauce. Vera loved cooking. Though she didn't do it often. Cooking for one was depressing. Occasionally, she'd invited the BAU team over and they'd shared a meal, which always ended in talking about a case.

She followed him into the kitchen where he began unloading the ingredients.

"I wasn't sure what spices you had, so I picked up what I needed." She playfully batted his hand away. "I'm the head chef here. And I don't need a sous chef, so go on that walk. Head to the chapel and I'll get all this going."

"You used to like cooking with me."

Her stomach knotted and heat flushed her neck and cheeks. On weekends in college, they'd taken turns visiting each other's apartment and dreaming up recipes. Mostly it was what to add to ramen to give it a more gourmet effect. After so many packages, it wore thin. But every now and then they'd splurge on payday and prepare something truly amazing.

Pasta carbonara with pancetta and spinach. Decadent chocolate cakes. And they'd dreamed out loud about how, when they had real jobs and less college debt, they'd eat like kings and cook together in the kitchen with a house full of kids whining about being hungry.

Things didn't always turn out the way one planned.

But she'd learned over the years that while she made plans in her heart, God ordered her steps and often those steps didn't match the plans of her heart. Sometimes they did, though. Really depended on what she was planning.

The kitchen grew quiet, warm and slightly tense. She forced a grin, shoving down fond memories. "I did like cooking with you. And I may still, but this is a gift. And you can't pay for half of your gift. Besides, you need some time out there to think." Brooks had always been a deep thinker and he did it best in the outdoors. A place he said he felt closest to God—surrounded by His beauty. "That hasn't changed, has it? Being outdoors to process and pray?"

"No. No, it hasn't."

"I'll text you when dinner is ready or if I need help chopping eggs for the salad."

"Then I'll try not to get too far back on the property. We lose cell service." He grinned and slipped out the French doors that opened to a large back porch and sweeping pasture beyond. From here she could see the small chapel's steeple. She'd like to venture inside herself. Pray. Feel the reverent atmosphere of a sacred place where many prayers had gone up, tears had been shed, and praise had been offered.

But for now she had work to do and it relaxed her. She simmered the sauce, prepped the salad and tucked it in the fridge, and by the time the lasagna was ready, the table had been set for three and everything was laid out and ready.

She hefted the four-layer deliciousness in the center of the table on a pot holder and Katie emerged.

"That smells good."

"It's gonna taste good too." Vera noticed Katie's red eyes and pillow crease on her cheeks. She knew that look well. She'd cried herself to sleep many nights. "Why don't you put ice in the glasses and I'll text your dad and see if he's stayed close to the house."

"Doubtful. He's probably in the chapel. You'll have to go get him."

Slipping out for a few minutes to see the chapel and another minute alone with Brooks wasn't the worst idea. She shouldn't want to though. Vera wasn't ever planning on a relationship again and he had pulled away from her. And he'd held her left hand. She couldn't forget that.

But she couldn't help herself. In Brooks's presence, she felt safe. Her insecurity was her own, she told herself. Brooks wasn't the kind of man to shy away from a scar on her hand.

He might not be able to stomach half her body riddled with them though. She had a hard enough time herself.

"Katie, go ahead and lock this door. Just precaution. You sure you're okay to be here alone a few minutes?" After hiding in the closet, she may not want to ever be alone.

"I'm fine. But I can't promise these croutons will be in the bowl when you get back." She grinned and popped a homemade toasted piece of bread in her mouth.

"I feel like that's fair." Vera darted outside and rubbed her arms. It was chilly and the wind seeped through her thin sweater. Thunderclouds rolled in and brought thick gray skies. The air felt wet with impending rain. Maybe she should have brought an umbrella.

She passed the fencing. Brooks must have put the few horses they owned in the stable to keep them dry. Nothing but pasture and brush. When she reached the stable, horses pawed at the doors and neighed. She inhaled the scent of hay and leather and horse manure.

The small A-frame chapel was about a hundred feet away, nestled in a patch of trees. Rows of stained-glass windows on each side and two thin windows flanking the front door. It hadn't been painted white, but was rustic wood. Perfect.

"Brooks! Dinner's—"

A boom splintered the air.

Not thunder.

Dirt surrounding her feet shot into the air.

"Brooks!" Vera dropped to her knees, pulled out the weapon she kept on her for precaution.

But the enemy was unseen. Lurking in the trees.

And she had no cover.

FIVE

Brooks heard the gunshot and sprang from the old wooden pew where he'd been pondering and praying. Gun in his hand, he rushed to the front double doors and, about fifty feet out, he saw Vera hunched on the ground with her arms over her head.

Returning fire into the woods, hoping to stave off the shooter, he hurdled the steps and ate up the ground to reach Vera. Panic lodged like a boulder in his throat and blood pumped hard and fast in his temples.

Another shot rang out and missed Vera, but now Brooks had a good direction to retaliate. He fired off two more rounds in the vicinity they'd come from, hoping it gave him time to grab Vera and run to safety. She was already up on her feet and hobbling toward him, using his gunfire as cover.

Thunder rumbled and a streak of lightning

split the almost night sky, which would work to their advantage if the lightning would cease.

As they reached each other, he grabbed her free hand as she fired a round with her gun at the tree line. "Into the chapel!" They raced inside, slamming the door behind them.

"Stay here. There's a back office where you can stay low. I have to go to Katie. You'll be safe."

Thunder boomed and the rain began to downpour, beating against the roof. He couldn't even text Katie to warn her to get somewhere and hide, that he was coming for her, but he gave it a shot anyway just in case.

He groaned and Vera snatched his hand. "You need backup. Katie can't lose another parent, Brooks. If you think I'm going to stay crouched in a dark room while you risk your life and Katie might be in danger, you have another think coming, sir. Besides, you can't guarantee I'm safe in here."

Vera was right. He needed backup for no other reason than he couldn't die on Katie, leaving her an orphan. But the thought of something terrible happening to Katie or Vera ran his blood cold.

"It's dark and storming. He's one man. His game is fire. If he was a better shot, I'd have already been dead. I'm ruling out professional sniper or military background. We have a chance."

"God, help us reach Katie and keep her safe," he mumbled, then he nodded once before he changed his mind, and Vera was on his tail. At the back of the chapel, he peered out the small window at the hall's end. The bell hanging from under the steeple lightly dinged from the force of the wind.

"The storm is a blessing, Brooks. Noise control. Blurred vision. But he might be lying in wait at the back door. We should go out the front. He won't be expecting that."

This woman was fast on her feet, her faculties calm and her gun steady in her hand. She'd been trained and was no spooked mouse, but there was a measure of fear in her eyes. "Okay. Let's do it."

Rushing while crouched low, they made it to the front door. Brooks opened it a crack and waited a beat. A gust of wet, cold wind blew inside and he shivered. "Now," he whispered.

Brooks went out first, his adrenaline pumping furiously through his veins. All he could concentrate on was getting to Katie. Vera was right behind him.

It was now or never.

Tearing across the terrain, they ran fast. Cold rain saturated his shirt and jeans, leaving his skin chilled. His hair matted to his head and rivulets of water streaked into his eyes and open mouth.

But they didn't slow.

Vera struggled but managed to keep up with his fast pace and long strides.

Past the stable.

Into the backyard.

Onto the patio.

The door was locked.

Brooks banged on it and yelled for Katie.

No answer.

Inside, the table was set family style and steam plumed from the piping hot lasagna.

"Katie! Open the door." Brooks had left his keys inside and he wasn't a fan of hiding keys outside. Anyone could find them.

Why wasn't Katie opening the door? He breathed a prayer and thought he might have a heart attack right then and there. Had the shooter abducted her? Was that why no shots had been fired on their run to the house?

"Katie!" Vera called.

Brooks grabbed his phone from his pocket now that he had a signal. The screen was wet and his thumbprint wouldn't open the phone. He entered the passcode. He clicked on Favorites and Katie's name came up.

He pressed her name and the call went straight to voice mail.

"She's not answering, Vera. She's not answering." Hysteria leeched his words and he couldn't help it. Didn't care.

"Okay, Brooks. Breathe." She knocked on the door again.

"Wait! There!"

Coming into the kitchen was Katie, as if she hadn't a care in the world, and he'd take it. Right now, he was thrilled she had no idea she was in danger and that her old man might have been dead in the pasture.

She saw them and frowned, taking her sweet time to the door. "Why are you hanging out in the rain?"

Caring less that he was soaked to the bone and dripping on the floor, he snatched Katie and hugged her against him. Vera closed the door and locked it.

"Eeew. Dad, you're wet and cold. Get a grip!" She wiggled out from his hold, her nose scrunched and a scowl on her face, and he laughed.

"Sorry. I just love you."

"Yeah, well, *just* say it. Now, I have to change, and I'm starving."

"Where's your phone?" he asked.

"Dead. I put it on the charger." She paused

and inspected his face, then Vera's, then returned her sights on him. "Wait. What's going on?" She pointed to the guns in their hands. "Is he back? Is he here?" Katie's eyes widened and she darted a glance to the windows behind them. "I'm getting my bow and arrow."

"Everything is okay, Katniss. You can relax."

Vera nodded her agreement and smirked at his *Hunger Games* joke. "I'm gonna make a phone call and get dry. Katie, can you put that lasagna back in the oven so it won't get cold?"

"Sure, but I know y'all are keeping something from me."

No point hiding it. And she needed to be alert. "Someone was on our property. We don't know if it was the arsonist."

"Yeah, well, who else would it be? Horse thieves?"

"Maybe," he offered and noticed the puddle on the floor. "I'm going to change." Vera had already left the room to call the Serenity Canyon police while he dealt with his daughter. "Stay away from windows. We can eat in the kitchen at the bar." So much for the nicely set table. It had been a while since he'd seen a spread like this. Sometimes Tracey brought by food or cooked up something but she was no gourmet chef like Vera.

Oh well. They were alive and together. Eating at the bar in the kitchen wasn't a bad thing.

"Do you think he'll come back?" Katie asked.

Brooks entered the laundry room off the kitchen and set the alarm code. "He's not getting in this house." Brooks's security was like Fort Knox. He'd paid the exorbitant amount to make sure his family was safe.

And yet he'd lost CeCe because of his own oversights. Not at an intruder's hand.

But would the shooter be back?

Likely.

Serenity Canyon police had swept the perimeter and cordoned off the chapel and surrounding area as a crime scene. Though the rain had washed away any evidence, including footprints, bullets had been recovered, so maybe a ballistics test would lead them to the gun owner and the shooter. Vera was hopeful.

Not wanting to ruin her big meal, Brooks had insisted they sit after everything had died down and eat at the bar in the kitchen. It had been quiet but not tense. Katie had eaten two pieces of lasagna and Brooks had helped himself to three. Guess adrenaline rushes and near-death experiences left a man famished. Vera had done her best to get one piece down, afraid any more would have lodged in her already tight throat.

She'd kept a cool head out there, been brave. That was the job. But now that it was over, her insides were mush. Thankfully, Brooks had good security. The killer had been on the property twice, but being locked up in here—with Brooks—gave her a measure of safety.

And Katie was unharmed. That was the important thing.

After dinner, Brooks helped clear dishes and load the dishwasher then Vera shooed him from the kitchen. Katie hung back and Vera had the impression she wanted to talk. She bagged the salad and covered the lasagna in foil then placed it in the fridge, waiting on Katie to get the nerve.

"I was scared," she finally said.

"When? Did you know what was really going on?"

"No. Not tonight. Since all this started, but after the other night. What if this person kills my daddy or you?" Katie's bottom lip was wedged between her teeth and her chin quivered.

Vera couldn't lie. Life was fragile to begin with and there were no guarantees. And she'd want candidness if it was her asking. "It's okay to be scared. I'm scared too. I suspect your father is as well."

She shook her head. "My dad isn't scared of anything."

Vera grinned as she hand-washed the skillet she'd cooked the ground beef and sausage in. "I don't believe that's true. I know he was scared when you didn't answer your phone or the door."

"Daddy gets concerned not scared."

She let it go. Katie clearly needed to believe her father was fearless.

"I saw him looking at you at dinner," she murmured as she sat on the stool at the island and plucked an apple from the bowl, picking at the little white sticker. "He likes you. Did he like you when you were in college?"

Didn't appear Brooks had told his daughter they'd dated; he might not want her to know. Great. Vera was backed into a corner.

"I knew it!" Katie said with a grin. "Your hesitation gave it away."

This kid really did need to grow up and become a detective or something.

"You were boyfriend and girlfriend, weren't you?" Kate propped her elbows on the bar and laid her chin on her fists. "That's cool. My mom had a college boyfriend. His name was Lars. Which I thought was kinda weird."

Vera chuckled, dried the skillet then placed it in the big drawer in the kitchen island. "Yes, we were. We dated the last two years of college. We'd met and chitchatted a few times in our sophomore year. Ran into one another at the library, got coffee. And it *was* cool."

"Why did y'all break up? Did he cheat? Did you?"

Vera snorted. This kid. "No. Neither of us cheated, but I wanted to go into the FBI and become an agent and he wanted to live here and work for the Serenity Canyon police. Good thing he did too. He met and fell in love with your mom, and without that, you wouldn't be here. And I'm glad you're here. The world needs you and your Sherlock Holmes-like abilities. Not to mention you're your dad's pride and joy."

Katie frowned. "I don't care. I'm still mad at him."

"I suspected. Have you told him?"

"I don't see the point." Katie reached across the bar and opened the glass cookie jar, snagging a butter cookie. How did she have room for one more bite?

"Helps to get the stuff out." She wiped down the stainless-steel cooktop, thankful it hadn't been a gas stove. Open flames did her in.

"Did you know I'm a Girl Scout?"

So she was done talking about it. Okay. Vera shook her head. "I was a Girl Scout when I was a kid."

"We have commonality." Katie grinned, smug at her understanding of the word. "Anyway, this

Friday night is the campout for my primitive camping badge. It's a...mother-daughter event." Her voice broke right along with Vera's heart. She wasn't even sure how to respond. "I'm not going, but I need the badge. I-I haven't said anything to Dad about it. He'll get sad and mopey, and he's finally not so sad and mopey anymore. Sometimes I think he should be and sometimes I think he shouldn't."

Vera laid the damp rag over the middle of the sink and sat next to Katie. "Why do you think he should still be sad, because you are?"

"No. It's nothing." She slid off the stool as the doorbell rang. Vera followed Katie to the voices in the living room. Tracey and Andy stood in the entryway, Tracey's hand resting on a rolling suitcase.

"Did you cook? I smell something delicious," Tracey said. "I'm famished. I hope it's low fat."

"I assure you it's not," Brooks said with a grin, "but it's the best meal I've had in a while. And there's plenty."

Tracey arched a perfectly shaped eyebrow. "Better than the chicken and rice casserole I fixed last week?" Her teasing had him chuckling.

"Slightly." He patted her shoulder and motioned her toward the kitchen. "If I'd known you'd be here, we wouldn't have put the food away."

"No worries. I should have called and said I was coming. We'll be sure to clean up again," Tracey said as she strode to the kitchen. "My stomach is growling like a banshee."

Vera headed for the fridge to serve Tracey and Andy, but Tracey beat her to it.

She removed the pan of lasagna and inhaled deeply as she lifted off the foil. "Yum. I really shouldn't be eating this though. It's going to add five pounds to the camera lens in the morning." She winked playfully. "But I'm gonna."

Vera took down plates and handed them over while craning her ears, trying to hear Andy and Brooks's conversation in the living room.

"Did you find everything okay?" Tracey asked. "Or did Katie help? She likes to be in the thick of things. So independent being an only child. I was too."

"I wished at times I was an only child." Vera laughed. "But no, it was easy to figure things out. Brooks is a creature of habit. Still keeps coffee mugs above the coffeepot and glasses nearest the sink for water. If I had to guess, I'd say he still folds his jeans instead of hangs them."

Tracey paused mid bite. "I believe he does actually. After CeCe died, he was a real mess.

Could barely get out of bed. I took a short leave of absence and tried to keep it together for him and Katie. CeCe wouldn't have wanted them to spin out of control." She laid her fork down without eating the next bite she'd cut.

"I know it was painful for all of you. CeCe was blessed to have a friend like you."

Her lips turned south and her eyes sheened with moisture. "Thank you. It was awful. We'd just been to a women's retreat near Big Bend. I had to get back early Sunday because I had work Monday at 4:00 a.m. and needed sleep. So we drove separate. Every day I wonder if I'd taken that Monday off and we'd driven my car if…" She shook her head. "I know that isn't helpful, nor will it change her tire blowing and her going over the ravine, but I can't help it. Andy's been my rock while I've tried to be one for Brooks and Katie. I remember being ten. Ten-year-olds need their moms. Now she's twelve and still needs her."

"So do forty-year-olds." Vera headed for the coffeepot. No one was going to go to bed early, so she chose loaded instead of decaf. "Though you wouldn't know that yet."

Tracey pushed her plate aside without even eating half her portion. "I'm older than I look. I'll be thirty-four in March."

"Thirty-four. Yeah, you're a real old lady,"

Vera teased as she made the coffee. "So you're engaged."

"Wedding this summer. I wished it would have been sooner so CeCe could have been my matron of honor. Then I made it clear I didn't want to be engaged right after her death. I didn't think it was a good decision to wedding plan immediately after what Brooks had gone through. Kinda felt like rubbing salt in a gaping wound."

"Brooks would have understood, but that's compassionate of you. Who will be your maid of honor now?"

"Katie." She grinned. "I want Katie right beside me when I say I do. It'll be like having a small piece of CeCe with me. She's really been lashing out."

Vera nodded. "With the shoplifting, I'm not sure—"

"Shoplifting?" Tracey's brows knit together and she pursed her lips. "When did she do that?"

"Today." Vera filled her in. "I'm sure Brooks would have let you know. It's been a crazy day."

"What else has happened?"

Before she could answer, Brooks entered the kitchen with Andy. Andy went straight to Tracey and rubbed her back. "You okay?"

"No. I would have liked to have known about Katie's escapade today." She handed him a plate of lasagna and salad.

Andy frowned. "I'm talking about Brooks and Vera being shot at a few hours ago."

"What?" Worry lined her brow.

Brooks told the sordid tale again. "But you'll be safe in the house. Security is set. Vera and I can protect you."

"Yeah, well, who is protecting you and Vera?" Tracey asked.

Brooks smirked at Vera. "We got each other's backs."

Thunder rumbled and the light rain turned hard and heavy again, pelting the roof while all sorts of emotions pelted Vera's heart. The way he'd said they had one another's backs felt intimate. More than watching out for one another professionally. It had been so long since she'd been a partner or on a team with someone.

She'd built a life then watched it burn before her very eyes. She wouldn't even know where to begin if she could rebuild. What would it cost to be vulnerable again? And with what she'd hidden behind swaths of fabric and long hair, the cost might be too much. The cost might be rejection again.

The coffeepot gurgled and the smell of French roast wafted into the kitchen, mingling with the lingering scents of tomato, garlic and basil.

Brooks's cell phone rang. He glanced at the screen. "It's Keegan." He answered.

What did the fire lieutenant want? Was it a friendly call or was it about the fires? Brooks bumped the air with his fist.

"Excellent... Yeah. Thanks. Andy, Tracey and Vera are here. I'll let them know... No, I hadn't heard. We had a little incident earlier... I'll tell you later... Wow. He didn't mention it, no... Okay. Thanks again, man." He ended the call. "Keegan found the metal bar used to trap Adrianna. He said it wasn't as burned as he'd anticipated, and there's a possibility CSI can find a print. But not to get too hopeful."

Vera imagined Adrianna's screams and fight to get out of the stable. She'd been in those shoes. Disoriented and turned around in her own home. Smoke thicker than the dust bowl. Blind to freedom. "What else did he say?"

"Oh, he said they were called out for the Jaws of Life. Car wrapped around a tree." His voice thickened. "The guy had overdosed. Looked to be a meth junkie. He wondered if Andy knew."

Andy had been narcotics. Small-town news traveled fast and crime news even faster.

"I actually heard that," Tracey said. "On the news scanner. Dom Martinez is covering it. Hon, did you know?"

"Actually, no. But I'm sure I will. Been some serious drug dealing overlapping from El Paso into the small towns. Bust over in Gran Valle about four months ago. It doesn't surprise me that it's reaching here to Serenity Canyon. Last I heard, there were some undercover DEA in the area trying to get the middle men so they'd lay down the big kahuna. But I've been out of the narcotics game a while."

Seemed to Vera like he hadn't lost his passion for it. "What made you leave narcotics?" she asked him.

"Until recently, homicide was safer." He looked at Tracey. "And I wanted to give my love peace of mind."

She kissed his cheek. "And you have."

Sacrifice for love. Vera could understand that.

"Look, I need to scat, but thanks for the dinner, Vera. It was delicious." Andy nodded at Brooks. "I'll let myself out. Call if you need anything."

Tracey walked him to the door.

Vera took their plates, but Brooks stopped her. "I got this. Go put your feet up. Rest." He brushed a hair from her cheek and held her gaze until the air swirled thick and warm with something Vera didn't want to define. She broke the moment, thankful she could escape under the guise of needing rest, even when she wasn't tired.

"Thanks," she said and scooted from the kitchen. She closed the guest room door behind her and leaned against it, breathing shallow. The blinds were open and she rushed over and closed them. But the eerie feeling someone was still out there, brazen and lurking, chased away the warmth of Brooks's touch and sent goose bumps up her arms and a shivery chill down her spine.

SIX

Smoke lingered in the air and Vera coughed and sputtered. Through dense, dark smog, a shadow approached. His hands covered her mouth and nose.

Vera's eyes shot open but paralyzing fear glued her to her bed. Disoriented, she struggled to get her bearings.

Brooks's house.

The guest room.

It had been a long time since she'd had a nightmare about the fire. Sweat slicked her body. Her pajama pants clung to her legs and the sheets were a tangled damp mess. This time the dream was different. There had been a shadow—the killer. The dream had felt so real, she could still smell smoke.

Not fire smoke, she realized.

Cigarette smoke.

Another cloud of fear enveloped her.

She sat straight up and a figure, like the

shadow in her dream, appeared like fog rolling in. Her feet were tangled in the sheets and she couldn't move fast enough, couldn't reach the night table for her gun quick enough.

He was on her, his body heavy but wiry. Dressed in dark clothing and a dark ski mask, his facial features and color of eyes were undefinable.

Wrapping gloved hands around her throat, he applied pressure and rasped, "You were supposed to take the warning and go. Now you're dead!"

Her throat ached from the force and her lungs burned for air as she clawed at his hands then reached for his face, digging her thumbs into his eyes. He drew back with a howl and she freed her feet, kicking him off the bed then rolling to the side and reaching for her gun.

"Brooks!" she hollered through the rawness in her throat.

As she grabbed the gun, the intruder dove through the open window into the night. Where he must have come in from.

"Brooks!" she hollered again as she moved to the window and hiked a leg out. Bruised ankle or not, she was not letting this guy get away again.

The door to her room swung open as she clambered into the night.

"He's out here!" She ran, wincing at the pain in her ankle. Brooks's footsteps were steady behind her. Rocks bit into her bare feet and the cool grass crunched underneath. The air was wet from rain and, up ahead, the killer was hopping a fence into the pasture.

Brooks passed her, gun in hand. "You okay?" he called.

"Yes." No.

Somehow an intruder got into a secured home. A heavily secured home. Knowing law enforcement with guns resided inside. That meant this man was unstable and willing to die for whatever mission he felt he was on. He was bold and reckless. But also smart and calculated.

She had no time to work the profile. About a hundred feet northwest, Brooks was at a stop. She jogged up beside him.

"I lost him."

Out here, it would be easy to do. Slivers of moonlight peeped between the dark shadows of night. Her feet stung and her heart was about to explode.

"What happened, Vera?"

"I woke up and he was in my room. He came through the open window." She briefed him.

"You had your window open?" His brow furrowed.

"No," she said breathlessly. "He bypassed security. How would he know to do that? Does he work for your security company or something? Who knows your codes?"

"Me. Katie. Tracey. Keegan." His eyes widened and his mouth fell open. He darted toward the house, leaving Vera in a confused, dizzy state.

"Wait!" She ran after him.

"Katie. Katie must have slipped out again."

Earlier she'd been angry at her father. Defiant in attitude after her stint with shoplifting then grieved over the fact that she couldn't go to the campout because she didn't have a mom. She might have taken off. She'd done it before.

Brooks practically dove back through the window and Vera followed, leaving muddy footprints on the hardwood, and ignored the throbbing in her ankle. Brooks stormed into Katie's room.

Oh no. Busted.

Katie stood in the middle of the room fully dressed, bow and arrow slung around her back.

"Where have you been, young lady?" Brooks asked.

Katie stood with her mouth open and eyes wide. "Nowhere."

"So you're sleepwalking with your bow and arrow? That's your defense?"

Katie zeroed in on Brooks's gun, and he shoved it into the back waistband of his sweatpants.

"I…"

No excuses.

"You could have gotten Vera killed tonight! *You* could have been killed tonight. How many times is it going to take before you realize that sneaking out for any reason is dangerous?" He stomped to the bookshelf laden with true crime books, snagged one then held it up. "You know these inside and out. They aren't fiction. These horrific events happened to real people. It isn't entertainment, Katie. It isn't made up. And before you say Serenity Canyon is safe and nothing bad happens here, look around, kiddo. Bad things are happening. People are dying."

Tears flooded her eyes, but she crossed her arms over her chest and dug her feet into the floor. Oh, the rebelliousness of youth.

"I didn't go anywhere…yet."

"But you disarmed the security system and an intruder got inside and nearly strangled Vera. *Strangled* her!"

"Brooks," Vera murmured. Katie didn't need to envision that. It was too harsh. Too much.

"No," he said to Vera. "She needs to know what exactly is going on and what she could have been responsible for."

Vera didn't argue. Katie wasn't her daughter.

But he was wrong. And angry. Later he would regret it.

Wide-eyed, Katie shook her head. "I didn't disarm the system!"

"You are grounded. Give me your cell phone right now," he demanded.

"But, Dad—" Katie whined and stomped a foot.

"No buts." He snatched the cell from her hand and blew out of the room, leaving Vera standing there with grass stuck to her wet, cold feet.

Katie glared at her, but tears rolled down her cheeks. "I wasn't outside tonight."

"Katie, it's hard to trust someone who's broken trust and lied before. Just today. And you are fully dressed." She noticed her shoes were dry. No muddy prints. No grass stuck to her, like Vera. If she had been outside, there would be proof. "I believe you haven't gone out. But you were going to leave, weren't you?"

Katie slumped on her bed. "Yes," she squeaked. "I wasn't running away. I just couldn't sleep and I wanted to go the chapel." She looked up. "I feel close to Mama out there. I wanted to tell her about my campout badge and how bad I want it. I don't want to earn it another way. I want to do it just like the other girls. At the mother-daughter campout. It's not fair."

Vera sighed and perched next to her, drawing

Katie close to her. She nestled against Vera and sniffed. "It's not fair. None of it is fair."

"No, dear one, it's not." The backs of Vera's eyes burned. "It never feels fair to lose the ones we love, especially too soon. I tried so hard to save my husband, Danny. But in the end, I failed. I lost him in our house fire."

"Is that why you have those scars on your neck?" Katie sat up and pointed to them.

Vera nodded. "I have burns on half my body."

"I'm sorry."

"Me too."

Katie wiped her eyes. "At least you didn't kill him. My dad killed my mom. And I hate him for it."

Brooks stood against the wall in the hallway, nails and hammer in hand. He'd been fully prepared to nail that window shut and even her door if that's what it would take to keep Katie inside and safe. She was putting her life at risk and everyone else's, but hearing those words…

My dad killed my mom. And I hate him for it.

His insides wilted, his stomach roiled, and tears bubbled in his eyes, burning and blurring his vision.

He had killed CeCe. By not changing her tires. By promising to and putting it off. Forgetting. And he hated himself too. But to hear

those words from his own flesh and blood…
She might as well have taken the hammer and
driven the nails straight into his chest.

She must have heard him talking to Keegan
about the tires. Or maybe she'd put two and two
together. It wasn't like CeCe hadn't repeatedly
mentioned they'd needed changing. He'd promised to get to it. Knew a guy who would give
him a deal. He'd handle it.

He hadn't.

When the tire blew, maybe his brilliant little
girl figured it out on her own. Either way, she
blamed him too. All her antics, her breaking
the law—she was punishing him. And hurting.

"Oh, honey," Vera said. "Your mom's death
was a terrible accident."

"But he was supposed to get her new tires.
If he had, she would be alive." Katie's hiccups
through tears unraveled him and he wanted
to go in there and cradle her in his arms like
when she was a toddler, but she wouldn't let
him. Didn't want him to.

"That might be true, but we'll never know.
I suspect your dad feels guiltier than you can
imagine, and that pain haunts him daily. He
wishes he could take it back, change the past,
and the fact that he can't aches like a bad tooth.
You know how I know this?"

"How?"

"Because a candle I forgot to blow out caught our house on fire. And it killed my Danny. Every day I wish I'd remembered to extinguish it. He'd be alive. I wouldn't have all these horrible scars and residual pain. But mostly he'd be alive and we'd have a family of our own." She sniffed. "I've never told anyone but my colleagues, and of course, the police and fire department in Quantico know. I'm telling you because accidents happen. That's why they're accidents. People forget, procrastinate, make mistakes. Not intentionally. And we pay for it."

"You didn't mean to leave that candle burning," Katie said. "You're a good person. I'm sorry."

"No, and your daddy didn't mean to neglect the tires. He's a good man. The best man I know. You need to forgive him. Danny would have forgiven me, so I have to forgive me, too, though some days are harder."

Brooks wiped his eyes with the back of his hand. Vera's words reached a deep place within him. If she could forgive herself, maybe he could forgive himself. CeCe would want that. She wasn't a grudge holder. Just like Vera's husband would have forgiven her.

God, forgive me. Same prayer he breathed daily even though he knew God didn't need to be asked repeatedly. What Brooks really meant was *Brooks, forgive yourself.*

"Vera?" Katie asked with a soft tone.

"Yeah, hon?"

"Do you think you could take me to the mother-daughter campout? I mean I know you're here to work and stuff, and you're not my mom, but you were a Girl Scout and… I was gonna ask Tracey, but… I mean I still can, I guess. I don't know. Never mind."

"First, you need to talk to your dad. Tell him about the Girl Scout badge. Tell him how you feel, maybe in nicer words, and then we'll go from there." Her voice cracked. She was moved. He could tell. "I'd love to take you if it's safe and doable."

"You would?"

"I would."

Brooks's eyes filled with tears again for so many new reasons. His baby didn't have a mom. And Vera was the most wonderful thing to walk through his door in two years. He backed out of the hall and Tracey stood nearby, a sad expression in her eyes.

She'd heard it all.

She loved Katie so much. "She's twelve and Vera and she have connected," he told her in a soothing voice. "Please don't take it personally. And at least she hasn't said she hates *you.*"

Tracey's smile was weak. "I know. I'm sorry you had to hear that. You have to know CeCe's death wasn't your fault."

"It kinda was. But…it was an accident."

"And the intruder? How did he get in?"

"He's gone. Katie disarmed the system." Guess she'd only caught the tail end of the conversation with Vera and Katie. "She was sneaking out again. She could have been killed."

Tracey laid a hand to her chest and eyed the hammer and nails. "So you're going to board her window shut?" She eyed him as if the idea was unwise.

"Well, I was. Now I'm just going to go sulk in my room. Do grown men sulk?"

Smirking, Tracey shrugged. "I think the word you're looking for is brood."

"Yeah, that's sounds more masculine."

He certainly wasn't going to sleep the rest of the night. He had a house full of women to protect. And he wasn't letting another one down again.

SEVEN

"We got a print from the bar used to barricade Adrianna in the stable," Brooks said as he entered the modest conference room at Serenity Canyon PD. He held two cups of decent coffee, both piping hot, and set one on the table next to a stack of files and reports that Vera had been combing over since nine this morning.

Her shoulders were slumped and her hair hung long, touching the table. She wore a pair of ice-blue reading glasses. Who would have thought they'd be needing those? When they were young and in love, there were only romantic notions of growing old together, which included grandkids running around, dogs playing and them on the front porch in rocking chairs. Backaches, stiff joints and poor eyesight never made the list.

Vera glanced up, her readers on the tip of her nose. "And?"

"I like how you go right to it."

Brooks sat at the head of the table, his leather chair wheezing at his weight. "Prints belong to a Salvador 'Sal' Dominguez. Last known address was El Paso. El Paso police are hunting him down as we speak. He's twenty-four. No priors for arson, but he has some petty larceny charges and one assault with a deadly weapon when he was nineteen. Nothing since. That's weird, right?"

Vera sipped her coffee, accompanied by a slight slurping noise. "Just because his print is on the bar doesn't mean he barricaded her inside. Do you know his last known job? Maybe he worked in a scrap yard or—"

"Construction."

"We definitely need to speak with him. If he can give us a list of jobs or places he's been recently, then we might be able to find a connection."

"If we can find him. He has no social media accounts. No paycheck. Which means he's likely being paid in cash. Not uncommon at all for contract work. El Paso PD says they'll talk to family and friends and keep us in the loop."

"If you don't hear anything in a few days, I know a Texas Ranger—Tack Holliday. He might be able to help."

"A Texas Ranger could definitely pull some strings."

"I hope so." She pointed to her files and laptop. "I've been looking at people who reported fires going back as far as thirty to forty years." She scooted him a piece of paper. "That list holds three locations within the fifty-mile radius of Serenity Canyon. More fires had been called in, but these right here are significant in my opinion."

Brooks scanned the list. Thirty years ago, three calls came in reporting three different fires set in Serenity Canyon Park within three weeks of each other. Each one escalating. A trash can. A bathroom trash can and the men's room caught fire. And then the wooden swing set. Each one was gasoline laden. "You think this is our guy just getting started with his fascination as a child?"

"Yes. Keep reading."

Brooks continued. Five years ago, a warehouse was set on fire. Two years ago, a pet shelter. Both using Molotov cocktails. Thankfully, no animals were hurt. An overnight tech had called 9-1-1 and got the animals to safety.

"You see the pattern?"

Brooks squinted. Looked back over the information.

"Threes, Brooks. He's obsessed with the number three. Three calls. Three weeks apart. Five years ago then two...five minus two is..."

"Three," he murmured.

"And these recent murders are three months apart."

"No one was arrested in the earlier fires."

Vera slid him another file. "No arrests, but one man was questioned. Harvey Roderro. He also worked as a tech for the animal shelter."

"Why did they suspect him?"

"The overnight tech had broken up with him three months prior."

"Three."

Vera nodded. "According to the vet tech, a Felicia Woodrow, Harvey was obsessed with fire and bombs. He would watch wildfires in California on the news with fascination. The breakup was ugly and she feared Harvey would hurt her. He'd threatened to make her sorry for ending things. Ultimately, they didn't have enough evidence to make an arrest."

"Where is Harvey Roderro now?" If he did try to burn his ex down in a pet shelter, he wasn't above these murders. "Does he fit the profile?"

"A little older than I originally thought due to seeing the attacker's hands, but I can't be sure. He's forty-two. Lives three miles from Serenity Canyon Park—his childhood home." She waited for that to sink in.

"Three. He would have been about twelve

when the park fires were set." Brooks's insides began to dance. This might be the break they needed.

Roderro would have lived close enough to carry a gas can to the park. Kids ran around without supervision back then and even now here in Serenity Canyon. "But where has he been between setting fires in the park and the warehouse fire? Or after he burned down the pet shelter?" If it was Harvey who had actually done them all.

"He went into the military at eighteen. Did two tours and lived in Arizona for a stint before coming back. Six months prior to the warehouse." She slurped another drink of her coffee. "I'm running down any fires with Molotov cocktails in the area of Arizona he lived. But he's back in Serenity Canyon now. In the same childhood home. His mom is under palliative care. Lung cancer."

"Is she a smoker?"

"She is. Lifelong. Many arsonists had a parent who smoked, giving them early access to tools to start fires like matches and lighters." Vera leaned back in her chair, crossing her legs and smiling with satisfaction.

"You are brilliant."

"I know, right?" She winked.

He laughed at her humorous false arrogance.

"How about we take a field trip? Go see Harvey Roderro. Shake him up a bit."

"I'm a fan of field trips," she teased and stood, grabbing her gray blazer from the back of her chair and gracefully slipping into it. She holstered her gun on her side and let the blazer fall over it.

Brooks's stomach roiled. "About you being a fan of field trips…" He hadn't brought up what he'd overheard last night between Katie and Vera. It had been too painful. He'd tossed and turned and prayed all night.

She slipped her purse strap over her slender shoulder and waited for him to continue.

"I, uh…let's get in the car and we can talk more privately." He opened the conference room door. Wary eyes met his but she nodded and followed him outside. Once inside the car, she buckled up and he cranked the heat to knock out the chill.

She rubbed her hands together. "What's going on, Brooks?"

"I overheard your conversation with Katie last night. I was coming to nail the window shut and—"

"You were not." She rolled her eyes and huffed.

"Well, I was angry and out of my mind. I'm not sorry about that. If that's what it takes to keep Katie safe, then that's what I'll do, and suffer her rebellion. But when I got there... I heard the part about her blaming me." Shame washed over him. "She's right," he mumbled. "I did, in a way, kill my wife."

Vera let a long breath release from her nose. "I'm sorry you heard that. She doesn't mean it. Not completely. And it was an accident, Brooks. If you thought the tires were an immediate danger, you know you would have done something sooner. I mean you're willing to nail a window shut to keep Katie in the house."

He tossed her a wan smile. "I didn't think it was that dangerous. I mean I knew the tread was thinning but I thought I had time."

"We all think we have more time. Until we don't." She twisted a ruby ring on her right ring finger. "I guess you heard why Danny died too." Her cheeks turned red and she stared at her lap.

"I did. You have no judgment from me, Vera. How could I? And I wouldn't anyway. Man, CeCe used to accidentally leave candles burning all night. She ended up trading them for those wax things that melt in little electric warmers."

"I wish I had done that. She was smarter than me."

Brooks reached over and tipped her chin. "I don't think any less of you. When I think about what you did..." His voice cracked. "Trying to save your husband, you're amazing. You've always been amazing."

"Don't make me out to be a heroine, Brooks." She sniffed and pulled away from his touch. "I'm not. But I appreciate you understanding."

"I do. Understand." He cleared his throat. "I also heard about the Girl Scout campout. I can't ask you to go. I know we have a huge case here and you're consulting but… I know it would mean a lot to Katie, and it might keep you both safe for a few days while I work. If Harvey is our guy and we confront him—"

Vera's eyes shone with moisture. "Brooks, you don't have to sell me on taking Katie to a campout for the weekend. I'd take her simply because I want to. She's a great kid. She's working through a really hard time and dealing with big emotions. Underneath all that, I see the lovely daughter you and CeCe raised together. You're a good dad and I know CeCe was a good mom. It's in the way the house is made into a home and in the brightness and sweetness of Katie. I would love to take her. We can't work 24/7. And yes, you're right. Getting her out of Dodge awhile wouldn't be the worst thing in the world."

Without thinking, he leaned over and wrapped his arms around her, inhaling her soft, sweet scent. Like flowers after the rain. Her silky hair tickled his cheek. It had been a long time since he'd hugged a woman, and places deep within moved and shifted and turned upside down. Been a long time since he enjoyed the feminine smell of shampoo and perfume, the feel of skin on his cheek and the way a woman fit right into his arms—like she belonged there, had been made just for his embrace.

"You don't know how glad I am that you're here. I thought it would be good because I needed help on this case, but it's more than that, Vera. You've been good for Katie. And if I'm being honest, you're good for me."

He felt her tense against him. Felt the slight rejection. He broke the embrace. "I didn't mean it like that. Not good for me in a romantic way."

"No, I didn't figure you did." Her words were short and clipped. "Of course not. I'm glad I'm here too. For the case and for Katie."

Whatever had swirled in the atmosphere evaporated. He'd said too much. Revealed too much. Scared her or maybe even offended her. As far as he knew, she hadn't had a relationship since Danny died and that was eight years ago. He was only two years in, and here he was hugging her and telling her she was good for him. She must think he was a shallow man.

"I'm sorry." He wasn't ready to move on. And now he felt the heavy weight of guilt for even entertaining the idea, for enjoying the connection between them. For appreciating her femininity. For allowing a longing for companionship to emerge.

"Don't be sorry. Let's get to work. We have a lot to do before Friday. I'm going to have to shop. I didn't bring camping clothes and certainly not for January in Big Bend National Park. But then, I knew I was coming to you, and you have always been adventurous. Seems Katie is too. Guess I should have prepared for any and everything." She chuckled under her breath and the awkward moment was gone between them.

But it was still lodged in his heart.

Harvey Roderro worked for Serenity Canyon Waste Management. He was tall and lanky, dressed in jeans and a dark green SCWM polo shirt. His brown hair needed a trim and so did his beard. Vera shifted uncomfortably but refused to tuck her hair around the right side of her neck though Harvey couldn't stop gawking at the burn scars unhidden by her blazer collar.

The fascination in his dark eyes curdled in her gut. Even more than hearing Brooks's tender gratitude at having Vera here. At first, she'd let Brooks's words seep into her bones, softening them.

She was good for him.

But she wasn't. Or she wouldn't be in the end. She had too many scars. Physical and emotional. Too many reasons to pull away and, in the end, she had. She'd also caught a small flicker of disappointment in his eyes or what she thought was disappointment, then he'd backpedaled, saying he didn't mean personally but professionally. She was good for him because she was helping with the case and his daughter. But she wasn't naïve. She knew what he'd really meant, and he'd been sorry he'd felt it and said it.

She had too.

But right now, they were in a tidy breakroom that smelled of lingering microwaved meals and burned coffee.

They sat at a six-person table in the corner by a drink and snack machine that hummed and tuned out the chatter in the hallway of the sanitation building.

Brooks had asked for Harvey's alibis for the murders of Lonnie Kildare, Wendy Siller and Adrianna Montega.

"I saw that on the news," Harvey said in a tenor voice, bypassing Brooks's question. "Burned up by the fire eater. That's what my mama used to tell me. Caught me once with her lighter. Told me the fire eater would eat me whole and to leave it alone but—" He stopped himself short. "Anyway, I never touched it again."

Lies. The obsession was so big, he couldn't help but talk about the fire. This could work to their advantage. Vera caught Brooks's eye, silently telling him she wanted to take over the questioning. He gave a slight nod and she shifted in her chair, hoping the movement wouldn't close her hair like a curtain over her neck. Harvey's fascination was disturbing, but it might intrigue him enough to keep talking.

"Good for you. Can you tell us where you were on those dates? Around 3:00 a.m. to 4:00 a.m.?" she asked.

Harvey shrugged. "Probably working. I can't remember. Shifts start at about four, though."

"We'll verify your time card with management. No biggie."

His eyes widened and she pretended not to notice. "Yeah, go ahead. But I might have been sick on one of those days. I don't know."

She simply nodded. "Tell me about how the fire ate the animal shelter where you worked."

Harvey huffed. "Place went up in blazes and they blamed me. Are you trying to blame me for the arson murders these past few months? I didn't have nothing to do with those."

"But you do like fire. You like watching it eat

up walls and doors, hear it popping and crack-ing as it devours. It's hypnotizing."

His eyes had dilated and his knee bounced as if he was trying to control the excited energy her words produced.

"It's not a crime to enjoy watching fire. It's a man thing." He pointed to her neck. "I see you've danced with the flames." He leaned for-ward, nearly salivating, and her throat turned dry. "What was that like? Feeling the fire lick your skin, melt your flesh?"

"That's enough." Brooks's sharp tone startled her and Harvey.

Vera wanted to bolt for the door. Run away and cry. Tuck her hair around her neck and maybe even throw up.

Harvey regained composure and sat back. "I didn't have nothing to do with those fires. And that's all I'm saying without a lawyer. Except this— It'll happen again. And again. Because some men can't be content to sit back and watch. Some men need to take an active part. Need to ask, 'May I have this dance?'" He chuckled under his breath and eyed Vera again.

"We're done here." Brooks stood. "Don't even think about leaving town, Roderro."

Vera paused, unsure if she could stand with-out wobbling. His questions had hurtled her back to the past, to the flames. The unbearable searing pain that had taken her consciousness at the end and Danny's life.

Finally, she stood and strode from the room without one glance at Harvey Roderro. Outside in the hall, Brooks pulled her into an alcove and gently grasped her shoulders. "Are you okay, Vera? I'm so sorry."

"For what? You didn't do anything. I knew this was an arson case. I'm fine." What a lie. She wasn't fine. But she would be.

"I didn't know he'd be so bold to bring up painful memories."

"He didn't bring them up, Brooks. They're always front and center. I can't escape them. Even if I were blind… I can feel them." Bumpy and ridged. She had no escape from the memories. Every day they were fresh. No smooth slate to work with. "But I've worked through them, for the most part. People look. Stare. And ask questions, which I don't mind too much."

"I wish I knew what to say. I don't. Maybe I shouldn't have been so selfish to call you in."

She appreciated his thoughtfulness. "I'm glad you did. Harvey Roderro is dangerous. He's calculated and cruel. He fits the profile. I don't know if it's him, but if it's not, it won't be long before he's committing homicide by arson. Maybe he already has and we just don't know it. I'd keep a close eye on him."

"We will. I'll let Andy know and Keegan. He'd be his worst nightmare—minus whoever is doing this."

Brooks's phone rang. "It's Tracey." He answered. "Whoa, slow down." He put the phone on speaker and held it between him and Vera.

"I got a note. It was on the windshield of my car. Andy brought me to work and then we had an early lunch and he drove me back to my place. I noticed the envelope on the windshield then."

"Is Andy with you now?"

"Yes. He's on the phone, calling in CSI, hoping there are prints around the car, or neighbors who might have cameras showing the street so he can get footage." Her voice was shaky and higher pitched.

"What's the note say?" Brooks asked.

"'Get ready to dazzle the cameras soon. Fire is your color.'"

Vera frowned. "It said 'fire is your color'?"

"Is that some kind of threat? Like he wants to see fire on me? Have me wear it?" she squeaked. "I thought we had more time before he struck again. This makes me think he's about to do something soon. I don't know if I can go back on TV live or report another fire he's set up."

Brooks sighed. "We don't know what he has planned, Tracey. Calm down best you can. Andy is on it and so are Vera and me. We may have a solid suspect. Tell Andy to call me as soon as he can."

"Who is it?"

"Tracey, now is not the time to go reporter on me. You know I'm not telling you."

"Fine. It's just my life at stake. What if your suspect has been entering my personal space and I don't recognize him as dangerous? I need to know who to be looking out for. I won't air it. I promise." Near hysteria echoed in her voice and Vera nodded. Tracey had a point. If it was Harvey and he was getting close to Tracey, following her…she needed to know.

"Harvey Roderro. That name ring a bell?"

"No. Not at all."

"I'll have Andy get you a photo so you can be aware. We don't know it's him, but he's a firebug, to say the very least."

"Andy's coming."

"Put him on, will you?"

Brooks talked to Andy and told him about their questioning of Harvey. Andy was checking cameras, and the typed note in a plain white envelope was going to the lab for prints and any other trace evidence.

"It could have been Harvey. That note was left on her car either last night or early this morning before we interviewed him," he said to Vera.

She nodded. "The wording is odd for Harvey though. Doesn't match his voice. But if he's clever, he might be masking himself. Right now, we need to worry about the first part of that note. 'Soon,' he said. 'Soon' as in a couple more months or 'soon' as in three hours, days or weeks?"

"He's moving on his plans faster now."

"Because he feels he needs to. I'm here, and he knows I'm not backing down or leaving."

"Which mean you're in as much danger as Tracey. Maybe more. This campout couldn't come at a better time. You need to get away a few days. He might think you're out of the picture and hold off, which would give us more time to catch him before he kills again."

But they both knew that wasn't true. Nothing was going to stop this killer's plans. Not time. Not Vera leaving town.

Nothing.

EIGHT

Friday had finally approached, and tents had been set up in a large circle. Girl Scout excitement was palpable and Vera had to admit her excitement was too. Ages had passed since she'd camped under the stars. She'd been dating Brooks—an outdoorsman through and through. He'd introduced her to real nature and how to enjoy it. Ironic she was now camping again in Big Bend National Park with his flesh and blood.

Katie had been over the moon when Brooks permitted her to attend. He hadn't relayed how he knew about the trip and Katie hadn't asked. She was too pumped to care and had immediately started her grocery list to prepare her no-trash granola as part of the badge requirement. Vera had some prepping to do as well. Like finding warm clothes for camping primitively in January. Thankfully, it wouldn't be below fifty during the day. At night they were going to hit the low forties.

In all the hoopla, Katie hadn't had the tough conversation with Brooks, but Vera prayed she would. It wasn't healthy or productive to clog the heart with bitterness and resentment. It would fester and cause a spiritual heart attack. It had happened to her. But Brooks hadn't wanted to admit he'd eavesdropped and Vera agreed that when Katie was ready she would come to him. No forcing it. That would make it worse.

In the meantime, he was dealing with hurt and added guilt, which crushed Vera. She had felt her own personal guilt but to know someone she loved also blamed her... Hopefully, she'd find an opportunity this weekend to encourage Katie to be honest with Brooks so they could work through the conflict. She'd pray God would heal their hearts and help them stay strong. She could use some strength herself.

Camping wasn't for the faint of heart; Vera's new hiking boots were already causing blisters on her feet and her bruised ankle wasn't loving the new shoes either. But Katie had loved every second of the shopping and prepping and had even brought her bow and arrow along. And been strongly warned by the troop leader to not use it.

They'd carpooled down, listened to the rules,

and set up camp a few hours ago, then gone on a short hike before roasting hotdogs over an open fire. Vera hadn't been a fan and Katie had roasted one for her.

The sun had now dipped behind the mountains and with the last light went the last of the warmth. She'd bundled in layers and blankets and taken a seat among the chairs that had been set up around the fire. Some closer than others. Vera had added an extra blanket since she kept farther back in the shadows.

Once again, safety measures were covered for nighttime camping and they'd taken precautions with their food so as not to attract night critters and bears. No one was to leave tents alone. The girls all nodded and mumbled they understood.

After all that was cleared up, the girls took turns telling spooky campfire stories. Some were borderline ridiculous and some eerily similar to ones Vera had grown up listening to as a child. Like the one about the icky, icky man with the icky, icky fingers and the man with the golden arm. The escapee from the asylum.

It was almost Katie's turn and Vera had a sneaky feeling Katie was beyond the golden arm and icky man tales. Vera leaned over and whispered, "Keep it PG. No true crime tonight. We don't need nightmares and bed wetters."

Katie giggled and licked melted chocolate

from a s'more off her fingers. "And all this time I was debating on Ted Bundy's escape from jail or a tale about H. H. Holmes."

Wow, this kid was morbid in her fixation on serial killers. If she didn't become a detective, she could always give Stephen King a run for his money. "Maybe go with Big Foot or something like that. Let's keep bodies intact and rule out cannibalism, hmm?"

"Yeah, okay. Fine." Disappointment dominated her tone. "But nothing's scarier than real crime."

"Amen. So maybe let's not exploit it. It's one thing to be intrigued into the investigation and catching a criminal. It's okay to be fascinated because your brain won't wrap around how sick minds think. But taking pleasure in people's pain is going too far. Let's not glorify homicide."

Harvey Roderro came to mind. He'd clearly been doing that with Vera's scars, taking pleasure in her pain. Instinctively, she bunched the plaid flannel blanket around her neck.

"I know. I don't. Really, I don't. I feel bad for the families and victims. It's just…how can they do that to people? I can't help but keep reading."

"I understand. It's a dark world, Katie."

"All right, Katie," the troop leader said with

a dose of trepidation. Obviously, Katie's penchant for true crime wasn't a secret.

Katie told a wild tale of a man who'd been raised by bears in Big Bend National Park and believed he was one. He hunted campers late at night, ripping them limb from limb and gorging on them. So much for keeping intact body parts and ruling out eating flesh.

After the big scare had them shrieking, the girls clapped and cheered while the moms turned their noses up and frowned upon the gory details. One of the girls piped up. "Agent Gilmore. You know some real spooky stories, don't you?"

"If I'm not allowed to tell them, then she's not either," Katie said.

No worries. She wasn't about to do that. "I think it's best to stick with tall tales tonight."

The moms nodded and thanked her. No one wanted to know the dark truths out there, especially while secluded by trees and shadows. Things really did go bump in the night.

"But, like, you do what they do on TV shows for real," Allyson said. Katie's best friend shared her fascination for true crime and archery.

"I have more paperwork than they do on TV, but yeah."

A girl with chestnut hair raised her hand but spoke anyway. School habit. "My dad says you're here to catch the serial killer who uses fire. Is he the one who burned you?"

"Addie!" her mother scolded.

"What?" she asked. "What did I say?"

Vera sighed inwardly. It was bound to come up in a gathering of curious middle-schoolers. "No, he didn't. I was in a fire at my home. And like Troop Leader Tamera said, it's important to extinguish fires. That includes candles." Might as well make it a learning opportunity. "And it would be wise to have folding ladders upstairs so if you have to make a quick escape from a two-story home, you can."

The circle grew quiet. Then Addie spoke. "But you are going to catch this guy, right?"

"I'm certainly going to do my best." She only hoped it was enough.

"And you get to work with Katie's dad, and he's hot for an old guy," Addie said.

"Addie!" her mother shrieked again, but this time she was grinning.

"That's what you said too! Only not old."

Vera snickered along with the other moms. Looked like Brooks had been a topic of conversation among the ladies. She could see why. Not only was he rugged with gorgeous black hair and blue eyes, but his voice alone held all kinds of appeal.

Katie groaned. "Not this again. Gross, y'all.

That's my dad! But Miss Vera dated him in college, so you know."

Oh brother.

"Really?" a mom said with curiosity. "Was it serious?"

Vera elbowed Katie and she returned it with a doe-eyed innocent look, her smile holding all kinds of mischief. She got her eyes from her mother, but that smile was all her daddy.

Looked like the ladies were more interested in the Brooks Brawley badge than the primitive camper badge. This was not the topic she'd expected to discuss, but she went along with it. "It was. For two years, but it ended well." She gave them the short version of two people taking different roads and parting with sweet sorrow. Disappointment but not dissension. "Everything worked out for the best."

The mom next to her leaned over and whispered, "When the girls go to bed, I want the grown-up version of the story."

Vera chuckled.

After a few more spooky stories, the girls put out the campfire responsibly then headed for their tents. Vera stayed up a little longer with the moms, enjoying the conversation, even if she did have to reveal a bit more of the story, but it was kind of fun to have some women to chat with. Since Chelsey had moved to Texas,

Vera had been a little lonely for female companionship.

She was quiet unzipping the tent, unsure if Katie was asleep or not. But as she wiggled into her sleeping bag, Katie spoke.

"Sorry if I threw you under the bus earlier. Did they make you tell all sorts of stuff like kissing?"

Vera laughed through her nose. "It's okay and yes, but I'm gonna pass on regurgitating it to you."

"Nice. That's gross."

No. No, it was far from gross, kissing Brooks. Her stomach dipped at the thought. He hadn't been her first kiss, but he'd been the best. A sliver of guilt needled her. Danny had been a wonderful kisser. She hadn't once thought of kissing Brooks during her marriage. But now… now was different.

They lay quietly listening to the rustle of the evergreens and cracks and pops of nocturnal creatures pillaging the forest floors, the whispers of moms and daughters inside their tents.

"I wish you could stay," Katie murmured. "Like after you catch this guy."

Vera's lungs clenched; part of her wished the same. "I'll visit, and maybe your dad will let you come see me. I'll show you around Quantico."

"That would be epic." She waited a beat. "I wonder what Dad is doing tonight."

Probably pacing floors and worrying himself sick. "He's doing his job and working to keep us safe. You know, once he saved me from almost drowning."

"For real?"

"Yep. We were white water rafting here at Big Bend. Got into some tougher currents and I fell out of the raft. The river took me fast. I couldn't stay above water even with the life vest. Your daddy jumped in, even at the insistence to stay in the raft. I don't know how he fought that current, but he did. He wasn't going to stop until he reached me and pulled me from those drowning waters. Once he had me in one arm, he held on to a rock until they could haul us back into the raft."

And he'd told her over and over how much he'd loved her and couldn't lose her. That she was safe. He had her. Just hold on to him. She had. Oh, she had. But she kept that intimate part to herself.

"I should talk to my dad and forgive him."

"Yeah. You should," Vera murmured and yawned quietly.

"You know…if you and Daddy decided to love each other again, I wouldn't be mad. I don't think Mama would either. She used to make these big dinners and desserts on the weekends and she'd say, 'Let's make Daddy happy.' That's all she wanted. And I think if he loved you again, it might make him happy. So she'd like that. And you can cook, so she'd really like that. You could make those weekend meals for him."

Vera rolled onto her side, thankful for the cover of night to hide the tears running down her cheeks. She couldn't deny her feelings for Brooks. "Katie, that is the most generous thing to say. I care very much for your daddy. I always have. But… I don't think that's going to happen. We'll always be friends, though. And now me and you—we will too." Katie was mad at Brooks but underneath the pain, her love for him was abiding and deep. Working out hurt was always sticky and confusing. She silently prayed for Katie and Brooks.

"I'd like that," she said through a thick, sleepy voice. Good. Vera didn't want to continue the conversation. Instead, she floated to sleep, remembering that memory of Brooks rescuing her from the currents and professing his love for her. He hadn't needed to say it.

He'd shown it in his willingness to sacrifice his life for hers.

Vera's eyes shot open. What had woken her? It wasn't the campfire stories. She shivered inside her sleeping bag. Ugh. She was no primitive camper. The only lesson she'd learned so far was not to camp in January.

But she had heard something.

There it was again. Rattling. Raccoons or maybe a bear sniffing around a vehicle or the food, but they'd hung it in a bear bag and followed all protocols. Well, if killers learned to adapt to get what they wanted, why not bears and critters?

She shucked off the sleeping bag and quietly pulled on her hiking boots without waking Katie. Another thing of youth she envied: deep, uninterrupted sleep. She grabbed her gun. Minus Katie's archery equipment, Vera's gun was probably their only other weapon out here.

Would a SIG-Sauer even take down a bear?

There it was again.

Using her chin to clamp the flashlight in place against her neck, Vera used her free hand to slowly unzip the tent. Once outside, the chilly wind sent a shiver down her spine. She zipped the tent up and used the flashlight to survey the campsite. A set of eyes, reflecting the light, peeked out like part of a spooky story.

"Lord," she whispered, "please don't let there be a bear. I have enough scars."

Inching toward the vehicles, she heard her boots crunch the dry grass and brush underfoot.

No movement or sound came from the tents. An owl hooted. As she neared the dumpsters, she shone the light, keeping several feet away, and spotted the bandits crawling over the cans in search of a late-night snack.

Raccoons.

Shoulders now relaxing, she sighed and shivered again. The sleeping bag wasn't doing it for her. Before leaving Brooks's house, he'd tossed in a wool blanket in spite of Katie's protests they had all they needed. Perfect.

Katie could speak for herself. Vera tiptoed past the vehicles until she came to hers at the very end. She'd parked last strategically. Never knew when the case might call her away. She opened the back passenger's-side door and reached for the blanket and the promise of extra warmth.

A heavy weight fell onto her back, shoving her against the seat and her face into the wool blanket, muffling her startled and frightened shriek, and releasing her gun onto the floorboard. Was it a bear?

Hands shoved her head deeper into the blanket.

No, it was a man.

She kicked backward, hoping to knock him out of the car; she rooted around with her hand, searching for her weapon. He must have realized her plan and yanked her from the car by her hair, throwing her to the dark, cold ground.

Without light, she was blind. Where had he come from? How had he known she was here? His gloved hands clinched tight around her neck and his weight kept her feet pinned. She clawed and scratched, hoping not to wake anyone else and put them in danger.

Fear and adrenaline raced through her veins and her lungs burned, desperate for air.

"Miss Vera?"

Katie!

"Are you out here?" A flashlight beam was nearing.

Her attacker froze then released her. She jumped up but he was already racing toward Katie.

Vera couldn't see Katie—only the beam of light—but she heard her shriek.

He was going after her. Why?

Vera dove into the back seat, grabbed her gun and hauled off after the killer, fear driving every step as she ignored her bruised ankle.

Up ahead, she made out Katie's shadow. Running. Fast.

Vera gained on the attacker and sprang into action, diving on him and knocking them both to the ground. "Katie, run! Run!"

Vera slammed the butt of her gun against the

attacker's head, stunning him. Then once more to knock him out. No choice. She had no cuffs, no way to restrain him for more than a few seconds.

"Daddy! Help us, Daddy!" She heard Katie hollering.

"Katie," Vera shouted. "It's okay. I have him."

Moms began to peek out from the tents, murmuring.

"Keep the girls in the tents!" She straddled the unconscious man's back. "But someone bring me a rope."

No one moved.

"Now!"

Katie came running, cell phone in one hand and a thin rope they'd used to hang their bear bag in the other. She froze as she approached. "Is…is he dead?" Her lip quivered and tears streaked her cheeks.

"No. Just unconscious. He'll be fine." But his victims wouldn't be. "You were supposed to turn in your cell phone. I saw you do it." She accepted the rope, shoved her gun in her sweatpants' waistband and went to work securely tying the man's hands behind his back.

"I did. But then I found the stash before we went to bed."

"The last bathroom break?" Vera asked, her heart thumping wildly as she moved to secure his feet, linking his tied-up hands to them like a roped calf.

"Yeah."

Of course, she did. "You should go back and stay in Allyson's tent with her and her mother. It's okay now. Did you…did you call your daddy?"

"Yeah, but then I lost a signal."

He was probably in the car on his way now, freaked out and worried sick, Vera figured.

Katie shone the cell light on the man and the ropes. "Nice constrictor knot," she said through a shaky voice. She was putting up a brave front, but Vera recognized a mask to hide fear when she saw one. She'd put on many. Brooks would kill Vera if she didn't force the kid back to a tent.

"Well, I *was* a Girl Scout." Though she wasn't sure she'd learned that knot in the troop. "Tent. Now."

"What's going on, Vera?" a mother called.

Now that the knots were secure, even if he woke, he was going nowhere. She stood and moved Katie back several feet. "We've had an intruder."

"Was he from the asylum?"

"The man with the golden arm?" two girls asked in unison.

"No." But he was icky. "Everyone stay inside

your tents and zip them. The area is secure. He's secure, but let's not risk a chance. I'll call the park rangers and let you know when you can come outside."

"Katie, give me your phone." She'd left hers in the tent and wasn't letting this guy out of her sight. "And you—"

"I know. Back to the tent. But, Miss Vera… you're a federal rock star." She hugged her quick and tight then went inside Allyson and her mom's tent.

Vera called it in, then Katie's phone rang again. The caller: Daddy.

She answered. "It's Vera."

"Why isn't Katie answering? Is everything all right? What's happened? I'm on my way! Is Katie safe? Are you okay?"

Questions fired faster than bullets. "Brooks! Calm down. We're fine. Everyone is safe and unharmed." Vera relayed the night's event. "Hold on." Who was this mystery man? Vera rolled the assailant over on his side and yanked off his ski mask.

She returned the phone to her ear. "I don't recognize him. Hold on again." She used the flash and took his photo then texted it to Brooks. "Do you? I just sent a picture."

Vera checked his injuries to make sure she hadn't bashed his skull in. He was bleeding but it wasn't terrible. Headlights shone on the road. Two sets of vehicles. "Park rangers are here."

"I'll be there in twenty minutes."

"Okay. Katie was shaken up. She'll need you." She kept her tone professional and calm but inside she was shaken up and needed him too.

"I'm not coming for just Katie," he murmured.

Brooks flew down the campsite road. The morning sun had barely begun to crack light into the world and two sets of headlights shone in the distance.

Brooks's gut was still in knots and his knees felt like water. Katie's voice had scared him half to death. He wasn't sure he'd ever been that afraid.

Except for once.

When he'd gotten word that CeCe had gone over the ravine coming home from the retreat. His brain hadn't been able to process it. He'd called her. Gotten her voice mail. Over and over, he'd called.

He'd thrown on some clothes and driven straight to the sight, terrified only to discover the news was true.

And CeCe was gone.

The memories vanished when his phone rang again. Tracey.

She'd heard the commotion in the house earlier and had been calling him for the past twenty minutes, but he couldn't talk. Could barely think. He needed to get to Katie.

And to Vera.

After parking behind the park rangers, he spotted the shadow of a man in the back seat of one of their SUVs. Vera stood between two rangers, wrapped in a coat and draped in the extra wool blanket he'd given them.

He sprinted from his truck and raced to her, snatching her to his chest and holding her with all he had. She was alive.

She'd done her job, was talking with the rangers. The woman was tough, smart, resourceful. "Are you okay, Vera? You scared me to death."

"I'm fine," she said but didn't pull away. Her arms came around his waist and she squeezed. Good. He wanted his presence to bring her comfort. Needed her to return the embrace, the affection.

She raised her head and he looked into her eyes. Saw a small dash of fear in them, but resolve and calm. He kissed her forehead. Kissed it again and let his lips linger on her cool skin. It felt good. Right. He'd done this a million times in the past, but it was like feeling her for the first time.

A park ranger cleared her throat. "As I was saying, we're going to keep the rope. Evidence."

"Rope?" Brooks asked.

"Agent Gilmore apprehended the assailant and knocked him unconscious then roped him like a calf." She grinned. "We had to cut them off to cuff him." She patted Vera's shoulder, female admiration and respect glowing in the ranger's face. "Well done, Agent."

Vera nodded. "Thank you."

He had so much more to say, to admire, but he wanted to see Katie. "Where's my daughter?"

"In the tent by that tree, with Allyson and her mom." She pointed out the tent.

He cradled her cheek, gave her a look to let her know he wasn't leaving and they had more to talk about. He did, at least.

She nodded and he bolted across the campsite to his daughter.

"Katie!"

The tent unzipped and she bounded out and into his arms. He hauled her up like when she was a preschooler and hugged her, kissed her cheeks. "Baby, are you okay?"

Sobs erupted and she clung to his neck, tears slicking down his skin. "Daddy!" she wailed.

She never should have witnessed this. None of these girls should have. "Oh, baby, it's okay. Daddy's here." The same two words he'd said a thousand times. When she'd fallen off her bike, the swing, when she'd been sick with fever.

When CeCe died.

He let her cry it out. His brave girl who seemed more mature and older than a twelve-year-old but wasn't. She was a fragile, sweet girl who'd been scared out of her gourd.

Had the killer come for Vera or for his baby girl? He said the fire would dazzle soon. But why not set their tent on fire?

Thank You, God, he hadn't!

Once Katie's tears subsided, he continued to cradle her; she still fit, would always fit in his arms.

"Daddy, I'm sorry for being so ugly lately. Can you forgive me?" Her lower lip quivered and tears burned his eyes.

"Can you forgive me?" He prayed she'd understand what he meant, that he knew exactly why she'd been acting out.

She nodded. "I love you."

From *I hate him* to *I love you*. His insides grew and soared. "Oh, baby. I love you too. So much. It's gonna be okay. We're gonna be okay. I promise." Somehow, he'd see to it. Make it happen.

"I know." She squirmed and he took his cue to let her down. She wiped her eyes. "You should have seen Miss Vera. She literally dove on his back, like that feral cat in the horse stable that jumped on yours that one time. Like, she looked just like that cat. And boom! He was down and she was all 'Take that!' and then she hollered for rope and was wrangling him. It was so awesome, Daddy. And so scary."

"I know." He grinned. "I'm proud of you both." He rustled her hair.

"Go be the sidekick. Miss Vera is so the hero." Her smile held pride and he couldn't agree more. Vera was the hero. Not only for apprehending a criminal and saving his daughter physically, but she'd been the mediator to repair and reconcile his rebellious, angry daughter back to him.

That meant more than she could ever know.

Somehow he'd make it up to her too.

NINE

In the interrogation room at the Serenity Canyon precinct, Brooks sat beside Vera and across from Wiley Page, the man who had attacked Vera at Big Bend National Park. He was twenty-eight. Born and raised in El Paso but moved to Serenity Canyon two years ago, living right on the county line. He had several "possession with intent to sell" charges on him among three counts of breaking and entering.

His eyes were dark and hollow, his skin pasty and scabbed over from the constant picking. A terrible side effect from meth. His teeth also declared his usage of the horrible drugs. Black and some missing. His cheeks were sunken and his hair needed washing. The smell wafting off him was almost overpowering.

After he'd been arrested and questioned by the park rangers, Vera had stepped in with the authority of the FBI and had Wiley Page transferred to Serenity Canyon for questioning. Behind the glass, Keegan and Andy watched her and Brooks conduct the interview.

So far, Wiley hadn't talked but he hadn't asked for a lawyer either. He'd swigged down two soft drinks and eaten a pack of peanut butter crackers.

"Why did you attack Agent Gilmore in the park?"

"I needed a fix. She interrupted me breaking into the car looking for cash. That's all." He shrugged as if indifferent to the situation.

They were going in circles. According to Wiley, he hadn't killed anyone or started any fires. He was up at the park camping, though he couldn't tell them where or how he got to the site. No permits had been taken out or cars registered in his name. The more questions Brooks asked, the more frustrated he became.

Finally, Wiley cleared his throat. "I want a lawyer now. I get one of those free ones 'cause I can't afford to pay for one."

Brooks rubbed the knot of tension and irritation growing at the base of his neck and stood. Vera followed suit. She'd been quiet during the interrogation, letting him lead and rarely interjecting.

"Fine." Brooks left the interview room and Vera followed. Outside, Keegan grimaced and Andy had his head cocked.

"Insight?" Brooks asked.

"Doesn't seem stable enough to set the fires," Keegan said. "But I suppose you can't put anything past someone on drugs." He rubbed his scruffy chin and sighed.

"Andy?" Brooks asked.

"I don't know. I tend to agree with the fire lieutenant. But something about him seems familiar." He looked harder. "Name isn't ringing a bell though."

"I don't think he's our arsonist," Vera added. "He doesn't fit the profile. He isn't a fire bug. I don't think he was up there digging in cars for cash, but I'd buy it long before I buy he's our killer. He *could* be the one who attacked me early on though."

Unfortunately, Wiley Page hadn't admitted to the earlier attacks on Vera.

"We have several puzzle pieces we need to make fit," Vera said. "Sal Dominguez's prints are on the bar that barricaded Adrianna Montega in her stable. He, too, has a few priors. See if we can connect him and Wiley Page in or out of prison stints. It's possible Wiley lifted the bar from where Sal worked and used it to lock our victim in the stable then came after me. But he's not the killer pulling the strings, if it is him. Who knows, maybe he was up in Big Bend doing exactly what he said. He wasn't trying to get inside our tent. He was near all the vehicles and had I not gone out, he may have left us alone."

"Why did he go after Katie then?" Brooks asked. "Our killer may have been there for her as well as you."

"He's a tweaker, Brooks. She had a phone and she ran. He chased after her. For all I know, he was going to snatch the phone in an attempt to keep her from calling the cops. People hopped up on drugs don't think rationally. They're almost always paranoid."

Maybe the guy and the attack were random.

But deep in his gut, Brooks didn't believe it. "Andy, call some guys in your old narcotics division and see if any information turns up about Wiley Page or Sal Dominguez. The Big Bend rangers are going to let us know if they find a vehicle belonging to Wiley or if one is abandoned. He had to get up there somehow. Meanwhile, y'all get some sleep. It's been a long night."

Night had slipped into day and no one had slept. Brooks checked his watch. Nine o' clock on a Saturday morning. He was exhausted and Vera looked beat too. Katie was home with Tracey and he had a couple of uniformed officers doing drive-bys, but that's about all they could afford. Brooks should have let Katie have a dog all those years ago. A big scary protector dog.

"Vera, maybe we should go get some rest. Start fresh on Monday. You can go to church with us tomorrow. I think you'd like our pastor."

She nodded. "I'd like that. And, quite frankly, I'm exhausted and starving."

Brooks swung an arm around her as they walked through the parking lot to his unmarked unit. "I think I could rustle us up some grub." And that gave him an idea.

Fifteen minutes later, they were entering his ranch. Tracey and Katie were in the kitchen and the island was covered with biscuits, gravy, bacon and eggs.

Tracey grinned. "When you said y'all were heading home, we thought you might be hungry."

Katie grinned and poured Brooks a glass of orange juice. "Are you? Hungry?"

"Famished," Vera said and hung her purse on the back of the kitchen chair. "Smells wonderful." She snagged a piece of crispy bacon and clutched her heart. "Bacon makes everything better."

"That's what I said!" Katie said and grinned. Brooks excused himself from the feminine chatter and slipped into his bedroom, flipping open his laptop. In just a few seconds, he had what he was after. He entered his information, paid online and printed the tickets for two.

This was the perfect way to say thank-you to Vera, and he might have some underlying motives. He wanted to spend time with her alone when they weren't working. He'd called Andy to ensure he'd be at the ranch tonight with Katie and Tracey, then he strode into the kitchen where Katie was reenacting Vera tackling Wiley Page.

"Miss Tracey, it was epic. Like a linebacker taking down the QB. Unbelievable." She turned to Vera. "I want to be just like you when I grow up."

Vera snorted and smothered her biscuits in sausage gravy and pepper. "Be better than me, Katie. You're much smarter."

Tracey grinned, caught Brooks's eye and held up a full plate. He accepted it and thanked her. "So what's on the agenda tonight?" she asked. "Since we're all cooped up together, I thought maybe pizza and old detective movies."

Brooks did love the old noir movies. Used to watch them with Vera and kept a collection.

"Do you still have the ones I bought you for Christmas forever ago?" Vera asked through a bite of eggs.

"No," he said quietly. "I didn't really think I should keep gifts from old girlfriends after I got engaged to another woman."

Vera smiled. "Duh. Sorry."

"Nah, don't be."

Tracey's brow scrunched.

Brooks explained. "My love of old detective movies came from Vera. She got me hooked in college and it became our Friday night tradition."

"Take-out pizza could get expensive, so we used to buy the frozen two-dollar ones. Except by the time we bought enough to feed Brooks, we might as well have gone to the pizzeria." Vera snickered. "I'm game for movies and pizza though."

"Good," Tracey said and busied herself at the sink washing pans.

"Actually..." Brooks cleared his throat. "I heard a friend at work talking about an outdoor kitchen cooking class for couples last week. I went online just now and they had two spots available so I kinda went all presumptuous and purchased two tickets. It's a four-course meal that we cook together over outdoor cooking stations. I thought it would be a good way to say thanks for saving my kid's life."

Vera laid her fork on her plate and held his gaze. "It's been a while since we cooked together."

"I doubt it'll be frozen pizzas."

Her smile dazzled him. "We cooked more than frozen foods."

They'd cooked up dreams and a future together once. Until those dreams went in opposite directions. They'd also cooked up some sizzling kisses too.

"That sounds awesome," Katie said. "A date."

Brooks's neck flushed and heat filled his ears. "I didn't say anything about a date, Katie."

"Two people going out and doing something for couples is pretty much the definition of a date, am I right, Miss Tracey?" She looked for support from Tracey.

Tracey blinked several times, clearly caught in an uncomfortable situation. "If your dad says it isn't a date, it's probably not."

Katie waved her off. "I can help you do your hair, Miss Vera."

"Oh…well…"

Brooks sighed. "Anyway, do you want to go?" he asked Vera. "It starts at six thirty."

Vera averted Katie's insistent gaze. "I would love it. But what about Tracey and Katie? One of us should be here."

"Not to be a killjoy," Tracey said, "but she has a point. I don't particularly want to be alone."

"Andy's off tonight. I called to make sure he hadn't made plans for you two first. You didn't know that?" Brooks asked.

Tracey's mouth slipped open. "No. I thought he said he was working. Well, I guess that's settled." But she seemed upset. Brooks assumed she'd be okay with Katie, but again, that was presumptuous. "You better bring us back leftovers."

"Well, I'm going to rest up before tonight. I'm exhausted." Vera carried her plate to the sink. "I can help in here first—"

"No, no. I've got this," Tracey insisted. "You go get some sleep. Besides, Katie and I need some girl time."

"Sweet!" Katie breezed to the sink. "I can finish my story about last night."

Brooks followed Vera into the living room and lightly grasped her forearm. "Now that we're alone and you're not on the spot, are you sure you want to go? It's not a date. Katie's just… Katie."

Vera stiffened. "No, I didn't assume it was. Besides, I'm already involved."

Disappointment struck him like a one-two punch to the gut. He hadn't expected that. Or the way it made him feel. A weird streak of jealousy raced through his bones. Who was getting all of this wonderful woman's free time? Hearing her laughter, running his hands through her hair while watching old detective movies on the couch. Who was embracing her when she was afraid and holding the privilege of encouraging her to keep at her job when it felt thankless? Who cooked with her in the kitchen and had the thrill to see her eyes dance with joy at his presence?

"Oh. I—I wasn't aware."

She cocked her head. "Didn't think I could find a man?" she teased, but there was something deeper behind her eyes. A sliver of hurt?

"No. Of course not. You just never mentioned—"

She breathed a laugh through her nose. "Stop backpedaling, Brooks. I'm messing with you. I'm involved—with my job. We're practically married. I don't have time to muddle through new relationships. Quite frankly, meeting new people and cutting through all the layers of falsehood to the real person sounds exhausting."

It did. First dates. Best impressions. Mixed signals. Blech.

"Tonight sounds fun. But I need a nap." She patted his arm and slipped down the hall to the guest room.

First dates did sound exhausting.

But he and Vera had known each other and been in love before. Seen the best and worst in each other.

So what did that mean?

After checking the weather app, Vera dressed in jeans, thick socks, her knee-length leather boots and a jade sweater that gathered in folds around her neck. The shade matched her eyes. She left her hair down, used an iron to create some beachy waves, then she grabbed her brown leather coat that matched her boots and glanced once more in the mirror.

She wasn't a spring chicken. Lines formed around her eyes and her lids weren't as smooth. She'd said goodbye to pencil eyeliner two years ago. But if she kept her sleeve on her right arm down far enough on her hand and her collar in place, no one would know she'd ever been touched by fire.

Not until they looked closer. That, she wasn't allowing.

Besides, this wasn't a date. He'd made that clear, and so had she. It was a nice thank-you and reprieve from the stressful circumstances. Her mind knew this fact well. Her heart was having a little trouble with it.

Being here on the ranch with Brooks and Katie had unlodged a piece she'd tucked down deep. Brooks had always been an amazing man, but seeing him as a father, too, had made a mark on her. And there was just enough of him in Katie that she didn't have to wonder what it would have been like to have a child with him. Regret at putting off kids with Danny was hitting her hard.

She stepped into the hallway the same time as Brooks and his light cologne wafted toward her. Her stomach dipped and her chest tightened. He wore a blue-, gray-, and-black-plaid shirt with a black cardigan over it and dark dressy jeans and boots.

Whoa, he cleaned up nice.

His sight settled on her and a slow grin spread across his face. "You look amazing. How is it you don't age?"

"You know what they say about flattery," she said in a flat tone, but inside she was giddy. Too much time had passed since she'd received a compliment like this from a man.

"It gets you everywhere?" His blue eyes held mischief.

"Exactly." She winked and he held out his arm. For not being a date, it felt like one. She slipped hers through the crook of his and he escorted her into the living room where Tracey, Andy, Katie and her cameraman Ryan huddled on the couch, discussing what movie to watch. That seemed odd. But she didn't live here and had no idea if Ryan hung out often with them or not. Brooks didn't seem confused or surprised.

"Whoa, Miss Vera," Katie said. "You look like a model."

Vera could hug this kid and never let go. "Your dad says flattery gets you everywhere."

She frowned, unsure of Vera's meaning, but Brooks chuckled.

"You look pretty dapper yourself, Brooks," Tracey said and wiggled her eyebrows at Vera.

"I clean up pretty good." He brushed invisible lint from his shoulder and grabbed his wallet off the table by the front door. Vera had already noticed he wore his gun under the cardigan. She had hers in her purse.

Brooks snagged Vera's coat from her arm and helped her slip into it.

"Cook up something good," Andy teased and the sentiment wasn't lost on Vera. She and Brooks weren't cooking up anything but dinner. Romance wasn't on the menu.

"Hope you don't mind me crashing the party tonight? Tina broke up with me," Ryan said to Brooks.

"You know you're welcome here, man. Sorry to hear about the breakup." He looked at Katie. "We'll be late. Love you, Katie Bug."

"Love you, too, Daddy. Y'all have fun."

Brooks pointed to the door and nodded to Andy to lock it after they left. "Trace, set the alarm."

"Will do," Tracey said.

They slipped out and Brooks opened the door to the truck for her. "So how far away is this cooking class?" she asked him.

"About twenty minutes. It's at a dude ranch owned by a fancy-pants oil-and-cattle family in Texas. The Brighton family. I've never actually been out there before but I hear it's a pretty swanky place. Lots of scandalous rumors about the middle son. Beau Brighton—ladies' man. Black sheep."

"Sounds like a soapy nighttime show."

"I hear it is."

"Maybe we'll get a peek at him."

He glanced over at her and smirked. "Maybe it'll make me jealous."

She laughed at his easy banter and light teasing.

Twenty minutes later, an enormous ranch home came into view. Soft glowing lights lit up the place like a beacon in the night. They drove past the iron gates. The drive wound and stretched through pastureland, mountains making a gorgeous backdrop until they reached the actual home.

"Reminds me of something out of a movie." The home was bigger than anything she'd ever seen in person.

"They have cabins on the property for vacationers. Horse riding lessons, a cowboy campout, and this big outdoor area where they've set up kitchen stations."

"I hope we're not making cowboy casseroles." Vera turned her nose up.

"I doubt we'll be making foil-packet meals and baked beans." He chuckled and a valet came and took his truck, then they were escorted on golf carts across the property to a large bricked area where individual cooking stations were set up. Soft music played from hidden speakers, a huge pool with floating lanterns provided ambience, and underneath a raw wood pergola, tiny white lights twinkled. Inside a huge brick fireplace, a blazing fire burned. She swallowed hard at the flames. A romantic notion, but these days Vera couldn't find flames attractive or a mood-setter unless the mood was anxious and fearful.

Other couples mingled and chatted as they snagged flutes of champagne served by men and women dressed in black-and-white uniforms. Excitement buzzed in the air and then a woman in her midthirties graced their presence. Regal and commanding, she wore an expensive and stylish black-silk jumpsuit and spiky heels that clicked along the brick floor. Behind her, a man a little older followed, dressed in a three-piece suit that fit tight around his biceps, and he wore his light-brown hair a little long. His rich brown eyes surveyed the room. His gaze held boredom but his smile was kind and a little arrogant.

Brooks leaned in and whispered, "If you start ogling Beau Brighton, we're gonna have to leave early."

Vera grinned. "You're safe." Beau was a gorgeous man, but she'd seen his type before. Nope.

"Welcome, everyone, to our couples' cooking class. I'm CoCo Brighton and this is my brother, Beau. Tonight we're thrilled to present to you renowned chef Keiron O'Malley from the *Dublin Oven* show on the Food Network. Many of you have his Irish cuisine cookbooks."

"I love Irish cuisine," Vera whispered.

"I know," Brooks murmured back and held her gaze. "I recall you wanting to visit Ireland."

For a honeymoon.

"Did you?" he softly asked.

"No. No, we spent our honeymoon in St. Thomas. You?" They'd talked about staying in old castles and visiting places with delicious Irish food.

"No. Bahamas."

A round of applause came and a man who looked more movie star than cook stepped out from nowhere with a million-dollar grin—and equally expensive haircut. He gave Beau Brighton a man-hug and kissed CoCo's cheeks. "Welcome, everyone. We're going to cook up some delicious food tonight and I'm happy to be here with my friends and to walk you through it."

The Irish brogue did a number on her girlish senses and Vera found herself grinning. Brooks leaned in and whispered, "Remember what I said about making me jealous. Applies to this guy too."

She elbowed him in the ribs and snorted quietly at his teasing. Keiron O'Malley was handsome no doubt, but he didn't come close to Brooks in her opinion.

"Everyone, choose a station. I'll take the one up front. You'll find a selection of ingredients on your working stations and in the small fridge. Tonight we'll be making a bacon and goat cheese crostini, an Irish pub salad and soda bread—the recipe straight from my mam's cupboard—and classic shepherd's pie. And for dessert, brioche bread pudding."

They chose a station in the middle. "Brooks, did you know he was making shepherd's pie?" Her favorite.

"I did." He laid down the carrots he had in hand and grasped hers. "I wanted this night to be special. You deserve it. And we never made it to Ireland…who knew we'd have Ireland in Texas?"

A little piece of the dream they'd once dreamed. It was perfect. Stars in the open sky. Dark mountains like looming shadows in the distance. A romantic atmosphere and Irish fare to fill their bellies. She almost forgot she was there on a case and lives were being taken.

As Keiron instructed, she and Brooks worked together well, flowing with one another as a flawless team. They laughed, teased and talked about everything from books to rodeos. Like old times. It wasn't hard to make conversation. Wasn't hard to laugh, even when the real world was heavy with darkness.

The crostini was delicious, the salad, soda bread and shepherd's pie divine and the bread pudding decadent, especially since Brooks added a splash more vanilla in the sauce than called for. They sat at their wrought-iron table for two and finished every last bite.

The couples gave a round of applause to Keiron and several people made their way to chat with him, but Vera was perfectly happy to talk to the man in front of her.

"Want to take a walk down the lit path to the fountain?" Brooks asked.

Did he not want the night to end either? This was picture-perfect, and she almost wished she'd turned him down. It was going to be hard to walk away with so many feelings vying for her attention and trying to rule her emotional roost. "I'd like that."

He stood on her left side and she discreetly switched so her right side was nearest to him.

She caught his frown, but let it go. Guess she wasn't that discreet. He laced his fingers with hers and they casually strolled down the brick path, the wind blowing her hair and sending a little chill down her back.

"That was a lot of fun. Truth is, I haven't had fun like that in a long time." Brooks kicked at a stray pebble.

"I haven't either."

The beautiful but ostentatious fountain bubbled, sounding like a waterfall. Standing silently, they stared into the water as it splashed from one tier to the next then into the large round pool.

"Vera," Brooks murmured and she pivoted to gaze up at him.

"Yeah?"

"You'll never know how much it means to me what you did to protect Katie. I've always known you were extraordinary but…she could have died and I—I don't know how to thank you."

"Brooks, you don't have to thank me. And I wouldn't say I'm extraordinary. I'm pretty ordinary." Less than these days. Unwanted.

He framed her face and she fidgeted. His fingers might touch a scar and the night had been too perfect for him to become uncomfortable and for her to have to see it. But he held her gaze, hypnotizing her and drawing her heart to his. Her pulse spiked and her throat turned dry.

She didn't shy away when his lips met hers. Heat rushed her cheeks and tingled her nerves clear to her toes. There were hints of familiarity in his soft exploration, his gentle easy way, but it had been so long since she'd kissed a man besides Danny.

And yet this was entirely new to her. He pulled her closer and her arms slipped around his neck, the feel of his hair on her fingertips.

So gentle. So precious. Cautious with the undercurrent of a man who was at the tipping point of wanting more but knew how to restrain himself, to give and not be greedy. Vera fell headlong into it, hoping it would never end. She tuned out any fear and ran with her heart.

When oxygen was demanded, Brooks broke the kiss and lightly pecked her nose then gathered her hands to his lips and kissed her knuckles. She could hardly stand from swooning. Then he brushed back her hair and she jerked her hand free to close the curtain over her scars. She didn't want to ruin the moment.

"Vera—" he said but his remaining words died on his lips as a gunshot rang out and the top tier of the concrete fountain exploded into the pool of water.

TEN

Brooks jumped into action, tossing Vera to the brick pavement.

Another gunshot cracked the night air and shrieks echoed from the outdoor kitchen. Panic was going to cause further mayhem, but there was no way to tell the guests they weren't targets.

The bullet slammed into the bottom of the fountain and water rushed from the hole. Another bullet nicked the brick pavers near Vera's feet and she instinctively jumped.

Brooks unholstered his weapon; Vera had already fished her SIG from her purse. They scrambled to the far side of the fountain, crouching. Hopefully, they were concealed enough to make a game plan. Running up the sidewalk the way they'd come was out. It was a lighted path and they'd be open targets, not to mention they could get innocents caught in the crosshairs.

Their only other choice was to head east toward the stables. Find shelter there.

"Let's run for the stables," Vera said.

"I was thinking the same thing. Go!"

They bolted and Brooks hesitated firing toward the shooter. The ranch had entirely too many amenities and people milling around. He wouldn't risk injuring anyone.

Vera paused.

"Go. I've got your back. We don't have time to argue over who brings up the rear, but you have the sore ankle so…"

She frowned then sprinted toward the stables in the dark distance. Brooks kept right behind her. He reached into his back pocket for his phone and called 9-1-1, but already he heard sirens. Someone up at the main house or outdoor kitchen must have called too.

Another shot cracked the atmosphere and Brooks grunted, his upper arm burning like fire. He grabbed it with his free hand, feeling blood seeping through his shirt and sweater.

"Brooks?" Vera called and turned back.

He motioned her on. "Keep going. I'm fine."

Hair whipping in the wind, Vera pushed for the stables. Looked to be about five of them all spaced out in a line. Vera ducked between two of them. The interruption unsettled some of the animals inside, and snorting and pawing at the stable doors broke the eerie silence.

"In here," Vera whispered and they slipped inside one of the larger stables, the smell of hay, leather and manure hitting his senses. On the wall was a row of saddles, and several barrels of feed sat below. "Behind the oats. Or whatever might be in those tubs."

They slid in behind the barrels on the stone floor. The cold seeped into his jeans and his arm continued to burn and throb, but right now he couldn't worry about the wound. Had the shooter missed Vera or was he trying to hit Brooks?

The killer said he'd strike soon, and they'd assumed by fire. He hadn't tried to burn Vera—only attack and kill her as an obstacle. So maybe he hadn't been aiming for Brooks.

"Do you hear anything?" Vera asked.

"Nothing but the horses and sirens. You?"

"No. Maybe the police scared him off."

Brooks leaned his head against the wooden wall behind him. "I'm not willing to find out just yet."

"You've been hit, Brooks. Can you tell how bad it is?" She touched his forearm. "Let me see." She turned on her cell phone flashlight and tried to keep the beam concentrated on Brooks's wound. She winced then frowned. "I can't tell with your cardigan on."

"I don't have room to shrug out of it."

"Are you light-headed or dizzy?"

"No." He was ticked and worried and confused. He clasped her hand in his. "Vera, I'll be fine. Stop worrying."

"Stop worrying? Really? We're hiding behind barrels of oats from someone who might not just want me dead but you, and you want me to stop worrying? You are so hardheaded."

"I thought of that, Vera. He burns up his victims. He shot at me."

"His victims were unsuspecting and easy to target. You're not. You're not only aware of his ploy but difficult to catch in a secluded place. His plans have been sorely messed with by me being here. He's deviating. He's impulsive and frazzled."

"Which means he'll make a mistake."

"Or kill us both." She sighed and leaned her head against the wall.

"PS," he whispered, "you're hardheaded too." He laid his own stubborn head on hers and held her hand again, rubbing his thumb along her hand, then her wrinkled wrist.

She pulled away, tucking her arm farther into her sweater. "I hear voices."

A beam of light and footsteps approached,

then someone called out, "Serenity Canyon police!"

"Agent Vera Gilmore and Detective Brooks Brawley inside," Vera called and slowly stood, hands up. Brooks's wounded arm burned but he managed to hold up his arms until they recognized it was truly him and Vera.

After a search revealed the shooter had escaped, paramedics transported Brooks and Vera to the local hospital where he received three stitches for the graze. Then local police drove them back to the Double B Ranch where law enforcement was finishing up questioning staff and guests and CSI was still combing the woods. The scene was released after everyone had been questioned, including Brooks and Vera.

Brooks had refused Vera's offer to drive them home.

Home. As if it was their place. Brooks wasn't even sure what he was doing.

He did know that kiss had knocked his heart clear out of the park. It had been so long since he'd kissed anyone but CeCe.

There was no denying how kissing Vera had felt. Like an eagle soaring on a strong current in a cloudless blue sky. He couldn't say it had been impulsive because he'd been thinking about it for days, no matter how much he tried telling himself that it was betraying CeCe.

But that wasn't true. CeCe was gone. Brooks would always blame himself, but CeCe wouldn't. She'd want him to be happy. To move on when the timing was right. He would never forget her, or stop loving her.

Maybe it was time to move forward. Maybe he and Vera had a second chance. Another shot. How would it even work? Vera had always wanted to be an FBI agent and she loved her job in Quantico. The woman was great at it. She helped so many people and made a difference in this dark world.

But he was rooted here. In Serenity Canyon. His daughter's life and all she knew was here. He was jumping the gun. He hadn't even had one date without an attempt on their lives and already he was deciding on transfers and moves?

But he had to think ahead. It wasn't just about him. He had a daughter to think about. Nor could he lead Vera on in any way. It wouldn't be fair. She'd been through so much emotionally and physically.

She was married to her job. Meaning she'd never leave it.

"What are you over there thinking?" Vera asked as they pulled into the driveway at Brooks's.

Busted.

"Honestly?" He cut the engine and shifted in his seat, facing Vera. "I was thinking about that kiss earlier."

She averted her gaze and tucked her bottom lip between her teeth, which only fueled him with desire to kiss her again. "It's been a while," she murmured.

"Since I kissed you or since someone besides Danny kissed you?" The thought of someone other than her late husband kissing her sent a wild green streak through him. She'd had every right to date, to kiss someone else good-night, but the effect it had on him was visceral and it scared him how much he cared.

"I only dated once after Danny. It didn't work out."

"Well, I'm glad it didn't." He smirked and inched toward her. "Because you might be here consulting on a case but you wouldn't be kissing me." He moved closer and she didn't back away or flinch. "And I rather like kissing you, Vera. I want to do it again. Can I do it again?" he whispered.

Her answer was wrapping her arms around his neck, her fingers faintly touching the hair at his nape. It was all the answer he needed and he encircled her waist, drawing her into his presence and tasting hints of raspberry lip gloss and hope.

Brooks couldn't get enough of her goodness, her kindness, her generosity in this kiss. Vera had always been an admirable woman. Full of life and faith. This kiss infused him with hope. That maybe they could be something again. It was new and yet familiar—easy to slip from conversation to kissing. There wasn't any awkwardness or shyness.

No hesitancy.

Only two people who connected on deep levels, knew one another well, cared for one another, and maybe even needed each other.

She was wonderful with Katie, and his daughter more than adored Vera. That alone meant more than he could say, and all the words he couldn't express well in conversation, he expressed in this kiss. His gratitude. The trust and faith he had in Vera, not just as an agent who could protect his daughter and help with a case, but as a woman who was loyal and faithful.

His heart reached out and met hers, dancing until the music had to end. They couldn't stay in his truck and make out all night, though he kind of wished they could.

He broke the kiss, easily, gently. Regrettably.

Vera's eyes were clouded, but they searched his. He saw so many questions there. More questions than he had answers to.

"That was amazing. *You're* amazing." He

brushed her hair from her face and she flinched. He sighed. "Vera, I don't have a problem with your scars."

Tears shone in her eyes. "Maybe not now, not consciously. But you will. They'll be a visual struggle for you."

Why would she think something like that? Because they were a visual struggle for her? Did seeing them remind her of not being able to save Danny? "You did everything you could to save him, Vera. It was a tragic accident. Please don't look at yourself and see guilt."

She sniffed and looked away then smiled softly, sadly. "I won't deny the scars remind me of what was and what should have been but isn't anymore. They do. I've come to terms with that, found a measure of peace. I need God's grace every single day. But that's not what I mean, Brookie. You will struggle with seeing them. It's not just my neck or my wrist. It's almost fifty percent of my body, and at first you might be with okay with it. And then you won't."

That wasn't fair. "You don't know that. You can't say that."

"I do know. That's why I can say it. I'm not the same woman I was."

No, she was stronger. Braver. More gracious. Relentless.

"I'm not the same smooth-skinned girl. I'm not beautiful in all the ways your wife was."

Did she think he was simply skin-deep? She should know him better than that. "I'm not comparing. Maybe you shouldn't either," he murmured and touched her cheek. "Something is here between us. You can't deny that, Vera."

"Maybe it's nostalgia. It's not like we parted on tense terms. No one lied. No one cheated." She licked her lips, stared at her lap.

He refused to let her off this easy. His chest tightened and his gut clenched. Lightly, he tipped up her chin. "You think that was nostalgia? You think this is nostalgia?" He leaned in and pressed his lips against hers again, feeling the zing instantly at the connection.

At first she hesitated, and he prepared to pull away. He certainly wasn't going to force an unwanted kiss. But then she sighed against his lips and melded into him. The walls coming down. He trailed his thumb across her cheek and into the neckline of her sweater, touching the puckers that ran below her ear to her collarbone.

They didn't scare him.

She tensed.

"I'm not afraid," he whispered against her lips. "Don't be afraid." He pecked her lips then found the tiny pucker below her ear, pressing a gentle kiss to it. "I'm not going anywhere, Vera."

Relief escaped her lips and her shoulders relaxed as he placed another tender kiss to the scarred skin.

"I am afraid, though, Brooks."

He framed her face. "I am too. But not of your physical condition. That's the least of my fears." He smirked. "I'm afraid of letting you down. I let down CeCe. I'm afraid of loving someone so completely again. Life is fragile. But it's also short."

She leaned in and kissed him again. "You're right, Brooks. It's not nostalgia."

Grinning, he nipped at her bottom lip. "I know." After one more swelling kiss, he sighed. "We should go inside." He wished the night didn't have to end, but it did.

She laid her purse on the foyer table as if it belonged there. Maybe it would. Someday.

She turned to him, gave him a contented smile. "I'm gonna go to bed. Sleep on everything."

"Dream sweet." He swept her into one more kiss then left her to her room and went into his to clean all the grime from the stable away. Once he was settled in a pair of sweats and T-shirt, he plopped on the bed. This could work. Couldn't it?

A soft tap on his door jarred him from his thoughts. Katie? Was she afraid? He rolled off the bed and opened the door to Vera, standing in a fluffy gray robe. Fear and vulnerability blanched her face. She swallowed hard. "Can I come in?" she asked.

Why did she want to come in? She was a woman of faith and morals, but she was at his bedroom door in a robe and he was unsure...

She disarmed him with a safe smile. "I just want to show you something. It's nothing like that. I promise."

Relief ballooned in his chest. But a woman hadn't ever been in this room except CeCe. He'd never even allowed Tracey in to clean or bring a basket of laundry inside. It was his place. Private. Intimate.

This wasn't any woman though, and he opened the door wider. She entered and partially closed the door. He frowned, uncomfortable, but he trusted her. Trusted she had a good reason for it.

Vera glanced around his bedroom, no doubt seeing CeCe's touches in the vase of silk flowers on the chest of drawers and the green wreaths above the night tables.

"You said you weren't scared," she said in a small voice. "A small pucker under my ear or on my wrist aren't unsettling—to you. But you need to see. You need to know before you get my hopes up or your own."

She slipped out of her robe to reveal a tank top and plaid boxer shorts—completely modest but enough to show the serious scarring. She lifted her hair from her neck and did a slow turn for him to see what she hid, what she feared he'd reject.

After a full circle, she met his eyes, trembling. "It's not pretty. It's not soft. It's not smooth." No. It wasn't soft or smooth. She was riddled with red splotches and white puckers. "And I may have surgeries down the road. Depends."

He cautiously approached, closing the distance between them. His heart ached like shards of glass had shredded it. He ached for her pain, for what she'd gone through, for the insecurity and for the loss. So much loss.

But he was not afraid. Vera Gilmore was beautiful. Glorious even. His throat turned dry and he longed to show her how lovely she was, how unafraid he was. But he was also a man of faith and morals. A man of honor.

"Well?" she squeaked.

"I'm so sorry, Vera."

The door burst open and Tracey barreled in, then skidded to a stop as she saw them in a position that could be misconstrued. She gawked at Vera, mouth open and eyes wide. "Oh. Oh my... I didn't realize..."

Vera snatched her robe from the floor and hurried to cover herself, her cheeks blooming bright red. Tracey's tact had gone right out the window and a fierce need to protect Vera rose up in Brooks.

He stepped in front of Vera, blocking Tracey's view and the shock on her face from Vera. Her eyes met his. "Oh, wow. Um... I—I..."

"It's not what you think, Tracey." And she ought to know him well enough to know that.

She held up her phone, still trying to see Vera from behind him. Anger bubbled on his tongue and released in a sharp tone. "What is it that has you busting in my room?"

Tracey started and clamped her mouth shut.

Vera had braved coming in here to reveal her vulnerability and to try and push him away, if he had to guess, and Tracey's ill timing and irritating reaction had not only ruined Brooks's response to Vera but did exactly what Vera had expected Brooks to do—freak out and fall apart.

Tracey slowly raised her cell phone. "I just got a text. I went to show Andy, but he's not in your office."

Andy was going to bunk on the futon in Brooks's office for the night. He hadn't been on the couch when they'd arrived home, but his car was in the drive. Where was he?

"It scared me. I wasn't thinking and I had no idea I'd be intruding on…something."

He owed Tracey no explanation. And he'd already told her it wasn't what it looked like. If she chose to fish for more answers or make assumptions, that was solely on her. "What's it say?"

"'In fire I'll consume you.'" She showed him the text. Probably from another burner phone. "I'm next, Brooks. He's gonna burn me alive!" She glanced over his shoulder at Vera, who was now completely covered, but Tracey had seen the ravages of fire. What it had done.

What it would do to her.

"Brooks, I'm scared!" Then she frowned. "What happened to you?" She pointed to his bicep, the stitches.

They hadn't called and told Tracey. She must not have been listening to the scanner per usual.

Brooks caught her up on the night's event. Vera remained eerily silent. "Let's go into the kitchen. No one seems to be ready for sleep tonight. I'll make coffee."

"I'll do it." Tracey gnawed at her thumbnail. "It'll help keep my mind off things." She hurried to the kitchen, leaving Brooks and Vera in the hallway.

"I'm actually going to go to my room," Vera

said, her cheeks flushed and eyes brimmed with moisture.

"Vera, you caught her off guard is all and—"

"No. I need to be alone. I *want* to be alone." She rushed into the guest room and quietly closed the door.

Brooks massaged the back of his neck. The night was a disaster. Vera thought he couldn't handle her scars. Tracey's killer had threatened her.

And where in the world was Andy?

Idiot. Vera had been so stupid Saturday night. First, she'd kissed Brooks, multiple times. Then she'd allowed herself to entertain the idea of falling in love with him and making a future. Her heart had taken her head hostage and driven her to a bright future with hopes of partnership, companionship and intimacy without fear.

Brooks had kissed her scar and proclaimed he was fearless, but she had needed to be sure. She couldn't risk trusting him and getting her hopes up, becoming vulnerable, only for him to change his mind. He needed to count the cost up front.

So she'd allowed him to see something no one had. After the devastation, she'd quit the gym and bought a treadmill. She no longer wore shorts, tanks or short sleeves. She kept her scars hidden. But in intimacy and full disclosure, all those hidden places would be exposed. He needed to know it so he had the chance to back out. Not that it wouldn't be a crushing blow now, but it would be far greater later if things progressed.

But the instant she'd revealed what she kept secret, she'd regretted it. Wished she could take it back. Then Tracey had rushed inside, halted by the horror and shock. It had been evident on her face, though she'd eventually attempted to mask it, but it was too late.

Humiliation had sent Vera hiding in her room Saturday night, and by Sunday morning, Tracey had been gone. She'd left with Andy who, it turned out, had been outside doing a perimeter check, which was why Tracey hadn't been able to find him when she'd gotten the text message. Vera had attended church with Brooks and Katie then eaten lunch at a café downtown. Katie had been a good buffer from the awkward tension, and Vera had been thankful for it.

After lunch, Vera had taken a long nap. They'd eaten frozen pizzas for dinner and when Katie went to bed, Vera had too. Brooks hadn't pushed or pressed to pick up where they'd left off Saturday night. What was left to say?

Now it was Monday morning and Vera found Brooks sitting in the kitchen with Tracey and

Ryan. Tracey had called in and taken off work but that didn't explain why Ryan was there. Other than his girl had dumped him and he and Tracey were friends. Vera cocked her head and studied him as she entered the kitchen. Ryan was a few years older than Tracey, but what did Vera know about him personally? Nothing.

Maybe she should remedy that. Look into Andy, too, for that matter. They'd been looking at strangers connecting with Tracey through the news. What if that wasn't the right angle? What if it was someone already close to her?

"Morning," Brooks said.

Vera avoided eye contact even though she could sense he was trying to make it. "Morning." She went to the coffeepot and poured a cup.

Tracey said nothing.

Once she added cream, she inhaled a deep, brave breath and turned, leaning on the counter. Today she was dressed in a black pantsuit with a scarf.

"I called Tack Holliday, my ranger friend, this morning. To see if they're any closer to finding Sal Dominguez. His prints on that bar have to mean something."

"I agree," Brooks said. All business. Good. Vera could handle professionalism.

"I want to look at Lonnie Kildare's murder

again," she said. "I know I keep beating a dead horse with him. But something feels off to me. Anything new with Wiley Page? You'd think he'd talk and try to make a deal." He was going down for attempted murder. He might not be the fire bug killer. But he might know something. And if he did, cooperating with the police would go a long way.

"What should I be doing?" Tracey asked. "I'm scared to leave the house. I definitely don't want to go back to my place."

"You can stay here as long as you want," Brooks said. "But not you, Ryan," he jested.

Ryan chuckled and popped the rest of a cinnamon-apple muffin in his mouth, crumbs gathering on his short beard. "I need to get going anyway. Since Trace isn't working, I'm covering for the afternoon shift. If anything else happens, though, let me know."

"Thanks for keeping me company," Tracey said.

Brooks walked Ryan out of the kitchen.

"Hey, about the other night…" Tracey said.

Vera swallowed a lump in her throat.

"I didn't mean to gawk. I probably wouldn't have, but I never expected to see you in his bedroom. I've never even been in there, other than Saturday night. He keeps it private. I was half expecting to see a shrine to CeCe. Any time

I've ever knocked, he always opens the door and steps out. So...to see you right smack in the middle of his...personal and private place, it was shocking, and then your robe was bunched on the floor and I knew you'd been on a date..."

"Brooks isn't like that. And neither am I."

"I know, but you were in the room. That threw me off."

Brooks allowing her into his private place meant something. "I understand. You were shocked and then to see what you did...it's shocking to see."

"Why, if you don't mind, were you letting him see? What *was* going on?"

"It's complicated. We have a deep history, one that didn't end on a sour note. And things are... developing. And that's all I really feel comfortable saying, Tracey. It's private and personal. Like his bedroom."

Tracey didn't hide her disappointment at failing to get the scoop. She was a reporter, after all, but she didn't press. "It's been really hard since CeCe died. Brooks hasn't dated anyone. Picking up the pieces has been tough. I don't want to see him hurt."

"Neither do I. I have no intentions of hurting him." If anyone was getting hurt, it would be her, if even unintentional.

The back door swept open and Andy busted inside. "Wiley Page is dead."

Brooks entered the kitchen and frowned. "What's going on?"

Andy said it again. "He hanged himself with his bedsheets early this morning."

Vera slumped in her chair. "Was he on suicide watch? Given any indicators of ending his life?"

"Not that I know of. I'm sorry, Brooks. Doesn't look like you'll be getting any answers now." He rounded the island and wrapped his arms around Tracey. "Don't worry, babe. We won't stop until you're safe. I promise." He kissed her cheek and she closed her eyes.

One dead end after another. Time was running out. The killer had an endgame.

To send Tracey up in a blaze and to kill Vera. Maybe his plan was to kill them all.

ELEVEN

"Say that again?" Brooks said through the line.

Principal Broadmore repeated his words. "I'm afraid Katie was caught red-handed stealing another classmate's AirPods. This is her third strike, Detective Brawley—actually, her fourth. I'm afraid we're suspending her for two weeks."

Brooks ran a hand through his hair and gripped onto it, silently praying for mercy and for God to tamp down his temper. Hadn't they made things right—him and Katie Bug? She loved him. Said she never should have been angry with him. He'd expected her delinquent behavior to end. But here she was getting suspended for stealing expensive earbuds from a classmate. What was she thinking? Better yet, why wasn't she thinking at all?

"You'll need to pick her up immediately."

"Yeah." He blew a heavy breath. "I'm on my way now." He ended the call and groaned. His chest constricted and his neck and shoulder muscles had tightened like screws. A head-ache was coming on quick.

Vera entered the conference room with cof-fee in hand. "What's going on?"

"Katie either took back her forgiveness or she's… I don't know." He explained the phone call. "I have no idea what to do."

Vera placed the coffees on the table and folded her arms over her chest. "I don't know. I thought she'd made some emotional strides. Would you like me to talk to her?"

Yes. But it was his place. His responsibility. He'd keep praying for God's wisdom. He had none of his own. "No, but thanks. I'm going to run and pick her up, and I guess bring her to the station. Tracey changed her mind and decided to go in to work." Against his wishes. An officer had been stationed there for the day shift. "So I don't have a babysitter. I have a ton of work right now. I don't need this."

"We can work from the ranch," Vera offered. "We have everything we need online. We can take the whiteboard I saw in your office the other day. What other choice is there?"

"I have other work to attend to. This isn't my only case. It's just priority right now. I have to be in the office."

"Then be in the office. I can work from your place, keep an eye on her."

"You're not a babysitter."

"No, I'm not. But we don't have a lot of options, Brooks. Unless your captain will make an allowance the next couple of weeks." She sighed. "I don't understand why she's doing this."

"Join the club. I'll be back after I pick her up. Broadmore stressed the word 'immediately' so... I need to be immediate."

"Don't strangle her," she said with a small dose of humor as he grabbed his gun and keys from the table.

"I'm gonna jerk a knot in her tail is what I'm gonna do," he muttered as he left the room and headed toward his unmarked. He prayed as he drove across town to Serenity Canyon Middle School. Katie needed help.

He needed help.

His prayerful thoughts trekked to Vera. They hadn't resumed their conversation from Saturday night and a ripple of tension was still moving between them. But not enough to keep them apart or to keep them from working together on the case. What was Vera thinking about that night? About him?

Didn't matter. Right now, he had to focus on Katie.

He parked up front and strode into the school. The sound of children's chatter and the smell of school lunch and bleach permeated the atmosphere. The office was to the right and he entered. Katie sat in the chair, her head leaned back against the concrete wall and her eyes closed.

"Katelynn Rae," he said.

Her eyes flew open at the sound of her whole name. Principal Broadmore approached and shook Brooks's hand. They'd played on the same football team in high school. Sympathy radiated in his dark eyes and a fair amount of pity.

"Katelynn, I'll see you in two weeks, and hopefully with a better attitude," Principal Broadmore said.

"And less sticky fingers. I assure you she'll be a whole new kid by then." Brooks laid the stern on heavy and Katie swallowed.

"Yessir," she said and trudged out of the office and into the parking lot.

Brooks said nothing for the first five minutes of the drive, letting her stew in her guilty juices. That had always worked on him.

"Katie, I thought we had come to an understanding. Why did you take the AirPods?"

"I don't know."

"You knew you were on the verge of getting suspended. How am I supposed to do my job and make sure you're safe? You can't stay home alone. I have to provide for us. You understand that, don't you? We have to have money to live. I have to make that money."

Katie stared out the window. Said nothing.

"You're grounded. Again. No devices. No true crime books. No TV. Suspension from school isn't a vacation. For either of us."

"Are you taking the next two weeks off then?" she asked quietly.

"No, I can't take two weeks off, baby. Someone out there wants to hurt people we care about. He's killed people. I have to do my job and find him."

"But your job almost got you killed on Saturday and Miss Vera too! You were shot! I can't be home alone. You have to be home!" She folded her arms and he caught a tear leaking from her eye.

It hit him then. With wild force. Katie was acutely aware that one more issue and she would be suspended. She'd stolen on purpose, hoping it would force Brooks to stay home with her and keep him safe. Saturday's debacle had terrified her. His sweet, poor and criminally clever kid. He pulled into the precinct parking lot and cut the engine then shifted toward Katie.

"It's okay to be afraid. It's okay to want me home. But this is my job."

"Then quit." The tears came with strength and her bottom lip quivered. "He's going to kill you and then I'll have no one. I don't want to be alone. Just quit and let's move away. You're always at work anyway, even before a crazy fire bug came to town. Can't we just go away? Can't you just want to be with me more?"

Tears stung the backs of his eyes. Taking her hand, he kissed it. "I'd love nothing more than to take off with you, kiddo. I love you. But I can't leave my job. I have to pay bills, baby."

But his daughter was fragile and needed him. She was right. He'd been distant in his grief after CeCe's death, then busy to keep his mind from fixating on his guilt and the what-ifs. He'd inadvertently neglected quality time with Katie. And now this case was eating up every hour of his day. He had to fix it.

"How about this. As soon as we wrap up this case, I take a leave of absence." He had some savings and he couldn't think of any better way to spend it than on his daughter, who desperately needed him and his undivided attention. "We can spend time riding horses, hiking in Big Bend, and maybe we'll even go to Disney World."

"I do like Disney," she said with renewed hope. "But I don't want you to work this case anymore."

"You want Vera to do it alone? Her and Andy, who has more narcotics experience than homicide?"

"Vera's pretty kick butt," she said.

"So is your ole dad."

"You got shot." Her lip trembled again.

"I know," he murmured and drew her to him. "I know I did." He kissed her head. "You pray for me, okay? Every day."

"I do. I do, Daddy. But I'm still scared." Her voice quivered and she buried her head in his neck.

Oh, if only he could give her words of comfort, promises that he'd be secure. But that wasn't a promise he could make. His job was dangerous. It was possible he could get hurt or killed. Those were the chances one took in this occupation. But he also understood how terrified his daughter was. She'd lost her mom already.

"Maybe find better ways to tell me how you feel, Katie, than resorting to criminal behavior. I know you think I respond best to it, but that's not true." He kissed the top of her head again. "And you're still grounded."

"Daddy!"

"You stole. You need to understand the means doesn't justify the end. There are consequences for every choice you make."

She sighed into his chest. "Yessir."

Inside the precinct, he directed her to a bench where she could sit and then went into the conference room. Seeing Vera there, chewing on a pen and her reading glasses on her nose, pulled him up short. She was absolutely breathtaking inside and out. But now things had changed—in an instant. Katie felt neglected. And she had been in some ways. She needed him most and she had to be his top priority. That meant whatever was happening with Vera had to be paused.

His stomach clenched and his throat ached. This was going to be difficult. Excruciating. He'd just allowed himself to open back up, to feel again. He'd made promises and declarations.

Vera looked up.

"Well?" she asked.

He explained why Katie had stolen the Air-Pods and how he'd failed her these past two years. "I mean she's entirely too smart for her own good, but she's afraid, Vera. I could have been a better dad to her. I have to be a better dad."

Vera's smile was warm and kind. "We do the best we can with where we are at the moment. I understand."

Did she? Did she understand what he was saying? What it meant for the future?

"Vera, I know what I said the other night and I meant it. I mean it. My feelings haven't changed but... Katie has to be my first priority, and she needs me."

"Brooks," she said with more force and stepped forward. "I understand. It's best anyway. I don't know that we'd have worked out."

Not true.

"It has nothing to do with you. Nothing to do with what happened in my room."

Her tight-lipped smile and the distant look in her eyes revealed she didn't believe him completely. But arguing with her was like arguing with a concrete wall. His heart sank and his legs felt like oak tree trunks pulling him down. In just two days, all hope had been lost. Vera didn't even believe him. He had no way to make her either. He was at a loss.

"Let's just work the case, Brooks, and we can part with sweet memories. Again." Her voice broke on that last word and she hurried from the room.

But he didn't want to be left with only sweet memories.

He didn't want to part.

Katie caught his eye from the open doorway and tossed him a weak wave.

This was best. This was the right choice.

The only choice.

Vera had spent most of yesterday afternoon in Brooks's home office. After creating a makeshift command center and posting photos on the whiteboard, she'd gone back over the case files. The text sent to Tracey unsettled her as much as the note before.

In fire I'll consume you.

What did that mean exactly?

There was a piece missing; once she clicked it into place, it would all come into view. But her profile was complete, and that's what she'd come to Texas to do. Consult and create a profile. Her job here was technically done. And Brooks had made it clear that he didn't have room for her in his life.

She held no grudges against Katie. She did need him. Far more than Vera, if she'd even admit she needed him at all. She certainly didn't want to. Didn't want to get swept up in him.

But she had.

She continued to replay that Saturday night when she'd bared her heart by showing him her skin. His eyes had widened. There had been a moment of surprise and even if he'd said that wasn't a factor in his decision, it was hard to believe it didn't have some bearing even subconsciously.

No use prolonging her own pain. She'd let him know she was leaving for Quantico at the end of the week. The longer she stuck around, the more she fell in love with Serenity Canyon, the ranch, Katie… Brooks.

Brooks lightly knocked and entered. "Hey."

"Hey." She picked up the official profile of the man they were looking for. "Profile is done. Harvey Roderro is a solid lead, and if he's not your killer, he's going to be someone's killer at some point." She handed it over.

He stared at it then his eyes cautiously met hers. "Why are you handing this to me?"

"Because my job is done, Brooks. You called me to consult and profile an arsonist committing homicide. I did. I'll be leaving at the end of the week." The words pinched her insides.

"I know what I said about time with Katie, but I didn't mean you had to leave," he said in a desperate tone. It broke her all over again.

"I think it's best."

His Adam's apple bobbed at his hard swallow. He looked around the room, anywhere but at her. "I wish things were different."

"I know. Me too." She inhaled deeply and slowly let it release. "Now, I have a few more days, so let's try and cover as much ground as possible. Where are we on the texts and phone calls to Tracey?"

"Burners. No way to trace them."

Brooks's phone rang and he answered and listened to the voice on the other end. Vera couldn't make out the words but Brooks's expression was grim. "Are you sure?... Okay. Thanks. I'll head that way."

"What is it?"

"They found Sal Dominguez. He was inside an old abandoned home on the outskirts of town."

"Is he talking? Has he said why his prints were on the metal bar that barricaded the soccer coach in her stable?"

"No. He overdosed."

Vera's insides unsettled. "Don't you find it convenient he's found dead? Now?"

"Yeah, but he has drug charges and is a known drug user."

Vera's pulse spiked. "By any chance, could you get me his files? And Wiley Page—I know he's dead, but I'd still like to peruse their history and see if I can find a connection. It's odd he's dead too."

Maybe the puzzle pieces were starting to fit, but until she knew for sure, she'd keep her thoughts close to her chest.

TWELVE

"Vera! Wake up!"

Vera's eyes shot open as Brooks stood over her bed, eyes wild. "There's another fire. We gotta go. Now."

Slinging off the covers, adrenaline racing through her body and sending waves of nausea through her from being jolted awake, she swung over the side of the bed and grabbed her cell phone. It was a little past 4:00 a.m. Still dark out. "Tracey?"

"No call this time. News came over the scanner that there was a fire in Serenity Park. Keegan and his department are there now. Tracey and Ryan too, covering it. Andy's on site. Hurry and get dressed." He strode from the room and Vera rushed to throw on clothes, smooth down her hair and brush her teeth then she raced into the living room.

"What are you going to do about Katie?" She

couldn't be left there alone. It was too danger-ous. A killer had already gotten into the home once.

"I called Allyson's mom. She's on her way." He handed her a to-go cup of coffee. The door-bell rang and he threw open the door to a tired Carinne Beaumont holding her own insulated cup of coffee.

"Thank you for doing this. I owe you."

"Just go. I could see the blazes on the way over," Carinne said.

"Hit the stay button on the alarm in the mud room. To be safe."

Carinne's sleepy eyes popped with alertness. "That does not make me feel safe, Brooks." She shooed him out the door and nodded at Vera. "Go, y'all. Catch this creep."

They rushed from the ranch and jumped into Brooks's unmarked. Voices on the scan-ner faded in and out as she buckled up. "Why didn't he call Tracey? Leave a message? This feels off."

"He knows Tracey works the morning hours. He wouldn't need to call her."

"And yet…it doesn't sit right. He isn't hold-ing to his pattern." She braced herself as Brooks took a hard turn, his light bar flashing as he sped through country scenery, mountains still shadowed under a canopy of darkness.

"I don't know. Ryan called me first. Then I switched on the scanner. Heard the commotion. Heard Keegan. Everything's gone down in fifteen minutes and that means he might be there watching in the background. We could catch him. End this." Hope rode his voice, but Vera didn't feel it.

"Is there a body?" she asked.

"I don't know yet. They have to get the fire out first. The gazebo was lit up and it quickly traveled to the trees. It's been a pretty dry winter."

In the distance the sky was lit up as if the sun had risen. Orange, red and yellow. A heavy cloud of smoke hovered like a killer, ready to choke and smother and destroy.

Chills rose on Vera's arms. She hadn't been this close to an uncontained fire in a long time. The campfire was the first one she'd been around in years. Her chest constricted and she rubbed her clammy palms on her thighs.

"Vera?" Brooks asked in his low baritone.

"I'm fine. I'll be fine."

Brooks parked behind the fire trucks, out of the way. The park was up in blazes. The firefighters were hosing everything down and Vera sat paralyzed as her past came reeling back.

Danny! Come on. Wake up. Oh, God, help me. The smoke had knocked him out, but he had a pulse. She couldn't believe she, too, hadn't passed out, but she'd been snuggled under the covers on that winter night.

Dragging him from bed, coughing and sputtering as her lungs itched and burned, she'd gotten him from the bedroom and to the landing, only to see the flames eating up their living room. She couldn't get him out through a second-story window. Flames already devoured the east side of the house.

The only way was down the smoke-filled stairs and through the fire.

Praying, crying, and her skin jumping, she'd raced into the bedroom, dragged the comforter off the bed and covered them up, then she struggled to get his unconscious body down the stairs. Once she did, the comforter caught fire. Sizzling heat. Torturous flames. Intense pain like nothing she'd ever experienced.

Vera had passed out.

Didn't even remember hauling Danny through the front door and into the yard. But it had been too late. The smoke in his lungs and the fire…he was gone.

"Vera, you can stay here. Stay here."

Brooks's voice reached through her memories and pulled her back to the present. Tears brimmed her eyes as she gazed into the fiery destruction eating its way through the park, the boats at the edge of the water, picnic tables. Everything disintegrating at its touch.

Brooks climbed out of the car, but she remained fixed in the seat, unable to move. Unable to push past the memories. She'd been unconscious for over a week before they could bring her out of the induced coma.

By then, Danny had been gone for more than seven days and she hadn't even known it. Didn't understand or remember fully what had happened at first.

Point of origin was the kitchen. We found glass from a candle.

The candle! She'd gone off to bed and forgotten about it. Somehow a spark had ignited a dish towel.

She shook off the dark thoughts and focused on the scene in front of her. Onlookers had gathered and cell phones lit up, filming personal video. Tracey stood in front of the gazebo reporting and Ryan filming. Police, EMT, firefighters. Other news cameras and vans. Park officials. The place was crawling with people.

Andy stood about five feet from Tracey, a grim expression on his face as he surveyed the crowd. Every few moments his sight wandered to the blazes the firefighters worked to snuff out.

And Vera sat like a scared little mouse inside the car while Brooks scanned the crowd and talked to other officials. She couldn't shut down. This wasn't her.

Forcing herself to open the car door, she inhaled the smoke and coughed. Memories lit up her mind and stole her bravado. She clambered back inside and closed the door again.

No. No she could do this. The killer might be out there watching. She needed to observe. Needed to do her job. Once more, she opened the door and this time she made it all the way out of the car. The air was cool, but it carried a wave of warmth from the fire.

She was outside. Everywhere an exit. She wasn't trapped or contained. She was in control. One step then another, she made her way through the crowd and met up with Brooks.

"What do we know?"

Her presence startled him and he studied her face, searched her eyes.

"I'm fine. Really."

Before he could respond, Tracey's reporting reached her ears. "We don't know yet if another life has been taken in this gruesome and all-consuming fire," Tracey said into the camera, her eyes aglow and face dewy. She had the hungry look of a reporter, like a consuming fire herself. Ryan grinned and nodded, urging her to keep going. "What we do know is the damage is irreparable here in Serenity Canyon and a person is responsible." She caught sight of Vera and Brooks. "Right now, lead homicide detective Brooks Brawley is on the scene." Ryan swung the camera around and the light blinded Vera. Brooks grimaced as Ryan and Tracey approached. "Detective Brawley, what can you tell us about this fire?"

Brooks's cheek twitched. "I've just arrived on the scene. I have no comment at this time."

"But do you think it's the handiwork of the man who's been leaving a string of bodies in his wake for the past six months?"

"No comment."

"How close are you to finding this killer?" she pressed. Did she not notice her friend was about to explode on her? She was doing her job but it was about to come at a personal price.

"No comment," he said with menace then blocked the camera with his hand. "I'm done here. I have a job to do." He motioned for Vera to follow and they turned their backs on Tracey and Ryan.

"I'm gonna kill her," he muttered. "I can't believe she's stayed quiet about her own direct involvement in the case. She can't keep her trap shut any other time."

Vera snorted. Police pushed back the crowd trying to slip under the yellow tape cordoning off onlookers. The gazebo had been put out and the fire was slowly being snuffed.

A balding man stood motioning for Brooks.

"Mayor. Be right back." Brooks jogged away from the tree line to talk with the mayor. As the fire was dissipating, the blanket of smoke grew wider, thicker. Vera shivered and rubbed her arms as she scanned the crowd.

There on the far side where the lake met the forest, she spotted a figure. Tall. Lanky. She unholstered her gun and crept through the crowd as the shadowed figure watched, unmoving, as they worked to extinguish the last remains of the flames. She pushed through a group of women gasping and commentating; the figure had disappeared.

He couldn't have gone far.

She inched through the darkness to the edge of the trees, pausing to listen, but the voices and water hoses were too loud to hear much of anything. As she switched on her Maglite, the figure burst through the darkness, toppling her to the ground, and her gun fell from her grasp.

"Let me see!" the voice growled. "I want to see." He rolled her over onto her back and Vera stared into the wild eyes of Harvey Roderro.

He pinned her arms above her head and tore at her blazer. She couldn't get her legs in position to kick as he straddled her, so she used all of her core strength and raised forward, surprising him. He loosened his grip and she headbutted him with so much force, she saw a spray of white lights in front of her eyes.

It knocked him backward and she jumped to her feet. The Maglite was on the ground, shining directly on her dropped gun. She grabbed for it but he tackled her again, shoving her face into the dried, brittle grass.

"Isn't it beautiful," he said with giddy fascination. "It eats everything. It ate you. I wanna see it. Wanna see the marks where it ravaged you."

She thrust her elbow behind her, connecting with his sternum, and reached for her gun again.

"Freeze." Brooks's deep, rich voice cut through the noise and Harvey obeyed. "Hands up where I can see them. Now."

Vera retrieved her gun and light and hurried to her feet, leaves and grass littering her clothing, which was in disarray from Harvey's sick fascination and clawing to reveal the burn scars. The guy was a sicko.

Vera pulled his hands behind his back, read him his rights through a shaky voice and cuffed him. Brooks hauled him beyond the trees and Tracey caught them. She and Ryan barreled through the crowd, beating other reporters to Brooks and Vera, bulleting them with questions. Brooks continued his no comment replies and hauled Harvey to his unmarked, tossing him in the back seat.

Andy approached. "Is it him? Is he the one threatening my fiancée?" He reached inside the car and grabbed Harvey by the shirt collar.

Brooks ripped him away. "Calm down." He shoved him back. "Cool off. We have no idea."

Vera wasn't so sure they had the man responsible for the murders, but she was 99.9 percent sure they had the culprit who'd started this fire. The interview with him may have set him off. His attack on Vera was likely a crime of opportunity, but they wouldn't know until they re-interviewed and investigated. His alibis for the other murders were murky. No proof he'd been home alone asleep on those nights. And his sanitation route went right by the station intern Wendy Siller's home. He could have sneaked off and set the fire. Somehow.

But he hadn't been in the shadows watching Tracey. His gaze had been fixed on the fire.

Vera had her doubts.

At the precinct, Brooks rubbed his itchy, burning eyes. The effects of the smoke still lingered. He smelled of it, felt it coating his tongue. He held a cup of coffee in his hand and paced the viewing room that looked in on Harvey Roderro.

Harvey hadn't confessed to anything but being an onlooker, though he couldn't deny his attack on Vera. He would be charged with aggravated assault on a police officer. That would get him locked up for a while, and if he was the killer, there wouldn't be any more calls or fires.

Tracey and Ryan were at the precinct, covering the fire and Harvey's arrest, along with other news stations from the surrounding counties. She'd put him on the spot. Put friendship aside for her job. He didn't blame her, but he sure didn't like it.

Keegan waltzed into the room, soot covering his face and still dressed in his gear, reeking of smoke, fire and sweat. "Hey, man," he said as he entered. He looked over at Vera, who stood quietly near the window, studying Harvey. The man had been obsessed with her scars from the first moment he'd laid eyes on her. Brooks wasn't sure how far he'd have taken it. One little peep at her neck surely wouldn't have been enough.

His stomach knotted at the thought of what could have happened.

"Agent Gilmore," Keegan said.

"Lieutenant," she returned quietly.

"We found the igniter. Molotov cocktail, but it was a jar instead of a bottle. Started at the gazebo. No victims discovered, but they still have some ground to cover." Keegan sighed. "It was a circus out there for sure."

Understatement.

"How long was the fire blazing before you got a call, and who called it in?" Vera asked.

Keegan rubbed his left earlobe. "Maybe ten to fifteen minutes. The gazebo was completely consumed and some of the dead grass was blazing near the edge of the trees. The call came from a woman who lived near the park. Winona Richardson. She was coming home from the night shift at the urgent care clinic."

"How many people were on the scene when you arrived?"

"We arrived in three minutes. Some onlookers, maybe a dozen at first. Then Tracey and Ryan arrived. That woman doesn't cower under pressure or stress, does she?" He chuckled. "After that, I don't know. I was busy doing my job."

"I noticed she did an interview with you after the fire was out," Vera said. "You're good under pressure too."

"It's my job. Like it's hers." He shrugged. "Anyway, I wanted to personally let you know that it was a Molotov cocktail. It's been handed over as evidence to the crime techs who are still out there."

"Thanks, man. Good job." Brooks clapped

him on the back and he left, leaving a scent of smoke in his trail.

Vera turned, her arms folded across her chest, her index and thumb pinching her chin. "Has he been interviewed by Tracey with each fire?"

Brooks glanced back at the door. "Not the first one at Twisted Shoe. Not his jurisdiction. But the other two before this one. Why?" He spun on her. "I've known Keegan my entire life. It's not him. You have no evidence to even prove it might be." How could she draw that conclusion? He knew her well enough to know she was absolutely thinking about Keegan as the killer.

"He understands fire better than anyone. The fires that killed our three victims were contained—unlike tonight. Tonight was a blazer, a free-for-all. Our killer didn't want to burn down the world or even the town. He simply wanted news. To incite fear. He just said Tracey did a good job—"

"She did."

"He has access to her personally through you, and you said they went on a few dates. That CeCe set them up. But Tracey met Andy—I'm assuming the man you referred to was him—and now they're engaged. How long ago did he propose?"

Brooks's stomach hiccupped and then sank. "Six months ago."

"When the first fire began." She laid a hand on his arm. "You're too involved. I'm not. We need to find out his alibis for the nights of the murders, and I'm all for being discreet, but, Brooks... Keegan could be a killer. He gets the limelight as the firefighter, while giving Tracey the story. It's like they work together. A hero duo. A team. A partnership. He wants no one to be close to her. But he is also harboring resentment for her rejection and then her falling for another man. The engagement could have been his trigger. A way of wooing her back to him...and maybe killing her if he can't have her after all this effort."

Brooks needed to sit down; he was feeling light-headed. "We need more than your conjecture." He raised his head and looked her in the eye. "If it's him, and I'm not saying it is, he wants her. Andy stands in his way."

"Which puts him in great danger if Keegan is our guy or not. We have to run every person and every angle." She frowned. "And if it is Keegan, we need to tread lightly. We don't want to tip him off."

"It's not him, Vera. This is crazy." He stood and dug his fingers into his hair. "Keegan is a good guy." There was no way he could be right under his nose and fool him. Brooks wasn't a rookie.

"Maybe. Maybe not. We have no choice but to go down every avenue. You know this. Not to mention, I'm leaving at the end of the week. You need my objectivity."

Leaving. The thought hit him like a sucker punch. But she was right. He needed her unbiased approach even if it revealed truths that Brooks didn't want to see. She made sense. Even so...he couldn't force himself to believe it.

Shaking his head, he gripped the back of his neck. "Vera, I know I'm about to sound like a broken record, but it's not him."

"Maybe not. In a small town like this it wouldn't be difficult to find out this kind of information. But we have to look at everything around us."

"How do we do it delicately?"

"That's tricky. Downside of a small town."

But they had to ride this road. And Brooks hoped and prayed his friend wasn't a killer.

THIRTEEN

"Brooks, I hope you're not too mad at me," Tracey said as she chopped vegetables for a salad and Andy stole a cucumber slice.

Vera coated chicken breasts with a marinade she'd learned from her grandmother. As she did, she thought back over the day. After the fire and discussing Keegan Lane as the killer, they'd visited the crime scene from the newsroom intern's death. Wendy Siller had gone into her shed and been locked in and burned. Wendy had been well liked at the news station and had a promising career.

But the killer didn't want to see her on TV. He wanted to see Tracey.

"You put me on the spot, and you know I didn't know anything and what I did know I wouldn't have been able to discuss on live television." Brooks sat at the table with a glass of iced tea. Katie was in her room reading books that weren't true crime. Those had been removed due to the grounding.

"I'm sorry. You're the one who said I should keep doing my job."

Andy chuckled. "Babe, you look amazing on TV. You're going to be an anchor before it's all said and done. You have real talent."

Andy sat across from Brooks, and snagged another cucumber.

Tracey grinned. "I don't know. Anyway, I was just trying to give you some air time. You've been working your tail off on this case."

"Not all of us need the limelight, Trace." Brooks shook his head and finished off his tea. "That smells really good."

"Lime and chili chicken." Vera slid the pan into the oven for the chicken to bake. "It will be."

"I like Harvey Roderro for these murders," Andy said. "I know he hasn't confessed. It's one thing to go down for a fire. Whole other to go down for three murders and several attempts."

"But Wiley Page attacked me at the scout camp."

"I thought you believed he might really be there pilfering through cars?" Andy asked.

"Maybe. It's possible. There had been a string of thefts. But Harvey lacks the patience and calculation. Our killer can wait things out. Time doesn't ruffle his feathers. He's a planner." She paused as a thought struck her.

"What is it?" Brooks asked.

"I think we may be looking at this from the wrong angle. Fire bugs are typically impulsive. The need to watch the fire burn. It's an urge that is uncontrollable. It's all about the fire. Harvey couldn't resist coming after me to see the damage the fire had done. He couldn't leave the scene. He wasn't in control. He's a real pyromaniac."

"You're saying whoever has been setting the fires might not be a pyro?" Tracey asked. "Why set them? Why talk about fire like it's their second love after me?" She shivered and turned her nose up.

"He wants us to believe it. To throw us off. The fire is a means to an end." Vera gripped the counter, her thoughts traveling at hurricane force. The killer was using fire, but the victims were more significant than the fire that murdered them. That wouldn't be the case for a true pyromaniac. Like Harvey. "I think our questioning of Harvey drove his impulse. Once we left, he fixated on fire. Couldn't help himself."

"You think it's our fault he set the park on fire?" Brooks asked.

"No. But I think we were the catalyst to get him going. I'm not putting any blame on us.

Harvey doesn't have what it takes to create a diabolical plan and slowly execute it. This takes someone with skill. Someone who has a keen criminal mind. Likely has committed crimes in the past and gotten away with them. He's obsessive. We may find crimes committed similar to these, like stalking, even restraining orders taken out against him."

"You're creeping me out, Vera," Tracey said and picked up the big bowl of Cobb salad she'd prepared for dinner. "I don't need some seasoned stalker to be infatuated with me."

No. She didn't. "I'm not trying to frighten you, Tracey. But we've been digging into the lives of those who are obsessed with fire. We've got to switch our approach."

Brooks reached over and stole a sliver of egg from the salad. "Does that mean you'll stay on longer?"

She'd already booked her flight home earlier this morning.

"You're leaving?" Tracey asked.

"I booked a flight to head home Friday afternoon. My job was done, but now it needs to be reworked. We need to start locally then work our way through the county and outward to find men who fit these criteria. He likely has charges and arrests, but no homicide—at least that law enforcement can prove. No real prison time. He's clever and slimy, sliding right through the cracks. I'd imagine these charges for stalking and probably peeping or harassment came in his younger years. Seventeen to twenty-five. We need to narrow it down. The older he gets, the more experienced he is at doing this."

"You think he's…" Tracey swallowed hard. "Killed other women before and gotten away with it?"

"Possibly." Or he may just now be working up to it with Tracey. But she kept that to herself rather than terrify Tracey further. She'd already done a pretty good job.

Someone like this wouldn't want to be on the outside watching. He'd want in close. Keegan Lane could still fit the bill, using fire because he knew how to safely wield it. The fires had taken three lives so far, but they had been contained to the victims alone. "Brooks, can I see you a minute?"

She left the kitchen and Brooks followed her. Once she was down the hall, she entered their makeshift command center. Brooks closed the door behind her. "What are you thinking?"

"Before you say he didn't do it, just tell me… does Keegan Lane have any charges against him or complaints for harassing women or stalking?"

Brooks sighed. "No." His eyes grew wider.

"Wait." He groaned. "When he was a senior in high school, he was all about Penelope Meggido. She wasn't into him, but he thought he could change her mind. He showed up at her house in a ploy to… I don't know…woo her? One of the rocks he'd used to get her attention broke her window. It ended with her dad escorting him off the property and calling Keegan's mom. But that was just dumb stuff. Penelope didn't fear for her life. She just thought he was a total tool. He was embarrassed and nothing like that ever happened again."

That Brooks knew of. He'd left for college and Keegan stayed behind. Who knew what he'd been up to the four years Brooks was away. "I still would like to know his history for the time frame I mentioned."

"So you are going to stay." Brooks grinned. "I'm glad."

"Only until I get a reworked profile. Maybe one more week or less. I can't… I need to go."

His mouth turned southward and he nodded. "I wish things were different."

"I do too." She slid by him, unable to discuss their dead future. Back in the kitchen, she and Tracey finished preparing dinner and set the table. Brooks called Katie to come eat and she entered the room with a pout. Grounding wasn't looking good on her.

She sat beside Vera. "Looks nice."

"Thank you." Vera passed the salad bowl to her and she helped herself to mostly bacon, eggs and cheese. Vera held in her chuckle. She had maybe four pieces of spinach on her plate.

"Dad, since I have no access to devices, I've been spinning my globe and searching for places we might go." Her tone was wooden and her eyes flat to drive home the fact she was bored to tears and over it.

Brooks ignored her dramatics, raised an eyebrow and heaped salad onto his plate. "Yeah? Where'd you land?"

"Morocco."

He laughed. "How about we keep it within three hundred miles, kiddo." He passed the bowl to Tracey and Vera laid a piece of chicken on Katie's plate.

"You're going on a trip?" Tracey asked through a bite of oven-roasted potatoes. "Now?"

Vera's cell phone rang. She didn't recognize the number. "Excuse me." She punched the green button and answered as she entered the living room.

"Hey, Vera. It's Ryan."

Why was Tracey's cameraman calling her? "What can I do for you?"

"Are you alone?"

She glanced around "Yes."

"Are Andy and Tracey still there?" His voice was low and urgent.

"Yes. What's going on?" She kept an eye toward the kitchen and wariness formed in her gut.

"I've been debating what to do all day. At first, I thought I might be ridiculous, but I don't think I am."

Vera pursed her lips. "Ryan, say it straight already. What is going on?"

"Look, can you meet me at the chapel?" He sounded scared, nervous. Why was he at the chapel? "I don't want to talk on the phone. Too many ears in the house. But I have information and something to show you. I don't want Andy or Tracey to get wind of it. He may already know."

She frowned. "He as in Andy?"

"Shh. Don't say his name. Just, can you come out here? I can meet you there in five minutes." Insistent urging had her curiosity piqued, but she wasn't going to go blindly.

"Fine. But give me ten or they'll suspect. Why didn't you just call Brooks?"

"He won't believe me. But I think you will."

"We'll see." She hung up. Was this a dumb move? Was this like a movie where the girl runs upstairs instead of out the door when a killer was chasing her? But at least she wore an ankle holster and her gun was strapped on. She pocketed her phone and returned to the kitchen. Resuming her place, she listened to the small talk and ate a few bites. When they finished eating, Brooks laid a hand on her shoulder.

"We'll clean up. Won't we, Andy?"

"Sure."

This was a great opportunity. "Well then, I'm going to take a little walk. Visit the chapel."

"Take a jacket. It's cold," Brooks said. She grabbed her coat and hurried outside, the wind sending a chill through her. She glanced back. No one was following. She made her way to the chapel and drew her weapon. Just in case. She was not gonna be that girl.

She slowly climbed the stairs and entered the front doors. Ryan sat in the first pew. He turned when he saw her, his eyes wide, frightened.

"Why am I here and not Brooks? PS—I'm not coming any closer and I plan to keep this gun trained right between your eyes."

Ryan held his hands up. "I understand, though I don't really like the 'bullet between my eyes' part."

"Again why am I here?"

"Can you tell me any reason why a law enforcement agent would need a burner phone?"

That wasn't a question she'd expected to hear. "No. Unless he was undercover. Why?"

Ryan slowly pointed to a gray bag by his feet. "Tracey asked me to grab her wallet from her gym bag when we were at the drive-thru after work. But I got into the wrong bag. I opened up Andy's gym bag instead."

"Why was Andy's gym bag in Tracey's car?"

"It's their new thing. Working out together, and Andy is on her 24/7 like a bodyguard since the murders. Point is, I found not one but two burner phones in his gym bag. I stole it. Neither of them knows. Yet. At least, I don't think they do."

Andy.

"You think Andy is the killer." He fit the profile. He'd inserted himself into Tracey's life. Stolen her away from Keegan—in his mind. He'd been her hero. Protecting her from the bad guy.

He'd worked narcotics.

"After I found it, I did a little investigating of my own. I don't plan to always be a cameraman, you know. Sal Dominguez and Wiley Page were both arrested on drug charges over two years ago. Andy Michaels was their arresting officer."

Brooks finished loading the dishwasher and ran it then poured himself a cup of after-dinner coffee, grabbed his flannel jacket and headed out to the back porch. He needed some thinking time. To process the new profile. Deal with the fact that Vera was sticking around but then leaving. Figure out what to do about his daughter. Katie was pumped over spending time with him. Much-needed time for the two of them. To heal together. Maybe time together would help her deal with his job and the danger of it.

The door opened and Tracey slipped out, covered in a big woolly blanket, a cup of coffee in her hand. "You look troubled."

"I am troubled, Trace."

"Talk to me." She sat next to him and patted his knee.

He blew a heavy breath and leaned forward, resting his elbows on his thighs, the warm mug in his hands. "After I lost CeCe...you know how low I was."

Her hand rested on his back. "I know," she murmured.

"I never once thought about another woman or even entertained the idea. It was too much. Too hard. But over time, I've been healing. Moving forward. What choice do I have, you know?"

"Moving forward is healthy, Brooks. CeCe would have wanted that."

"I know. But I haven't found anyone I wanted to move forward with. Even when I called Vera in for the consult, there was never an underlying motive to rekindle a relationship or any inkling of hope. It was just an old friend coming to consult. Only…only I did fall in love with her again. I didn't plan for it to happen. Didn't even want it to happen." But it had.

"Does she know?"

He nodded. "I mean she knows we have something. I haven't told her that I love her. I can't. She has her own reasons for not wanting to move forward. And then there's Katie. Katie's been acting out because she's been mad at me. And this last ordeal is to keep me safe." He explained why she'd gotten suspended.

"I can't devote time to any woman. Because the only woman in my life right now has to be my daughter. When this case is over—and I feel like we're making strides—Katie and me are going to take some time off. I'm going to take a leave of absence. And who knows, maybe I'll pull her from school—homeschool her the rest of the year—and we'll just do some traveling. Go to Disney. Maybe Morocco." He laughed.

"I don't know if traipsing off and pulling her out of school is a good idea, Brooks. She needs routine and stability. She needs to understand your job is important and you can't uproot simply because she wants that. Every time she wants your undivided attention, she might do something outrageous. You're only teaching her that she can get what she wants if she behaves badly." Tracey leaned forward to catch his eye. "I'm not saying she doesn't need you. She does. It's probably best to devote yourself to her. But to take her to Disney for stealing AirPods?"

Tracey had a point. Rewarding bad behavior was never sound or wise, but in this case, it wasn't about a child acting out and rebelling. It was a twelve-year-old motivated by fear of losing her only parent and doing a desperate thing. And time away might be good for them both. They hadn't gone anywhere since CeCe had died. They'd kind of died too. It was time to live.

"I hear you, Trace. You make a good point. But I do believe this is best. I just wish it could include Vera. Maybe someday it can. If she's willing. I don't know." He leaned back and glanced inside. "Where's Andy?"

"He went for a walk. Get some air." She stood. "I'm going to leave you to your thoughts. It's all going to work out."

He grabbed her hand and squeezed. "Thanks. We'll catch this guy. We'll keep you safe."

"I know. I trust you. I'm gonna lay down. I'm whipped. Physically. Emotionally. Mentally."

"I hear ya."

She slipped her hand from his and went inside.

* * *

"Why didn't you want to tell Brooks?" Vera asked. She tried to recall any information she'd been given about Andy. He'd transferred out of narcotics. He easily could have used criminals he'd put away with the hope of a get-out-of-jail-free card or he could have paid them in drugs. He'd know how to get access. Then when he'd met up with Sal, he'd killed him and made it appear to be an overdose. And who wouldn't believe it? The guy had previous drug charges. And he could have easily used another inmate to make Wiley Page's death appear to be a suicide—or maybe Wiley had ended his life on his own accord. He had a lot to fear from Andy, and that fear had motivated him to keep quiet in their questioning.

Andy knew they'd gone camping. Probably even knew the alarm code. Brooks trusted him. Tracey trusted him. Katie really might not have disarmed it after all. She'd fessed up to every other disobedient act.

But not that one.

Andy knew they'd gone to the cooking class. No one would suspect him. He could have used the excuse work needed him and passed Ryan off as protection. He was obsessed with Tracey. Calculated. Clever. Sneaky. Vera's updated profile was spot-on. Andy wasn't a fire bug. He killed those people for a specific purpose. To scare Tracey and keep her close? To get her to say yes to the engagement? Tracey'd even said she'd balked at the engagement to try and be compassionate toward Brooks with all his loss. Then the fires happened and a week later she said yes. Maybe the fires had been done to incite fear and the truth that life is too short not to keep going forward. To move on. To make the most of life's opportunities.

Vera hadn't.

She was walking away. Not taking Brooks at his word that her scars didn't scare him. They scared her. But did they scare her more than she loved Brooks?

Vera was tired of running. Tired of being afraid.

But it didn't matter. Brooks had made it clear that for now he needed to devote all his time to Katie. She still agreed. Neither of them knew the time frame. But maybe he needed to at least know that if things changed, and when Katie was healed and in a good place, she'd be around. She'd wait.

Brooks was worth waiting for.

Unless Katie was his cop-out. No. That was nothing but insecurity talking, lying to her.

Vera sat on the pew, ridding her mind of thoughts of Brooks and focusing on what Ryan was telling her.

"I didn't tell Brooks because he trusts Andy. Tracey is gonna marry the guy! I can't risk Brooks telling me I'm crazy and Andy finding out. Everyone he's used is now dead. I don't want to end up in the same boat." Ryan massaged the back of his neck. "So now what?"

Now what? Good question. How did they prove it was Andy? Burner phones and two criminals that he'd arrested weren't enough to charge him. It was enough to question him, but the second he realized they were on to him, he'd cover his tracks. Or something deadlier.

Likely he'd used burner phones to contact Wiley Page and Sal Dominguez. There would be no way to connect him. They needed to see if any odd numbers had come into Andy's phone recently. But the murders still bothered her. A stranger. Someone closer. Then even closer. Was that to make Tracey afraid Brooks or Katie was in danger? And why did he need her to fear that? Or was he trying to make her believe *he* could be the next victim in case she got cold feet? Even Vera had thought that might be a possibility. If he was a potential victim, Tracey would cling even closer to his side—where an obsessed stalker would want his fixation.

But why did he go all the way out to Twisted Shoe to pick a random victim? Why not eenie, meenie, minie, moe and light up someone's home in Serenity Canyon? Lonnie Kildare was a stranger—to Tracey. Maybe not to Andy! They hadn't entertained the thought that Andy and Lonnie might have a connection. Why would they?

"We have to tell Brooks. We also need to see if the victims can be connected to Andy. He had access to the last two because they were connected to Tracey. But what about Lonnie Kildare? Does Andy have ties to him or to Lubbock where Kildare was from?" Where was Andy from? Had he ever resided in Lubbock?

"I don't know."

"For now, pretend you have no clue what's going on. We don't want Andy to suspect or Tracey to get suspicious of your behavior. She's intuitive. Part of her job. Maybe even call in sick in the morning if you don't think you can play it off believably. When I get back to the house, I'll pull Brooks aside and fill him in. We'll go from there. Don't go digging, Ryan. Andy is dangerous."

He nodded. "Okay. Yeah. You're right."

"Keep out of sight. Where's your car?"

"On a back road about half a mile away. I came through the west side of the property."

She nodded. "Go back the way you came. Go on now. I'm staying here a few minutes." She wanted some time to pray and think. About the case. About Brooks. About herself.

Ryan slipped out the back door of the chapel.

Vera wanted phone records from Kildare. Easier to get than requesting Andy's. She didn't have enough to get that warrant. They didn't hand those out on hunches. She wasn't ready to tip off Andy either. She called the station to talk to the officer who'd been assigned to help her and Brooks with gathering information.

No service. Ugh. She forgot it was crummy at best.

She wandered the chapel, holding up her phone in random places. Found one bar and made the call.

"Hey, Officer— Hello? Hello?" She moved to the right.

"I can hear you now."

"Sorry I'm in a place with terrible reception. I need another favor." No response. "Hello? Hello?"

"Hello, I'm here."

She blew a frustrated breath and spoke quickly in case the call dropped. "Email me and Detective Brawley Lonnie Kildare's phone records. Sooner is better than— Hello?"

"I'm still here."

"Sorry. Did you get that?"

"I did."

"Okay thanks." She hung up and growled at her phone then made her way to the small altar steps and knelt.

Lord, help us with this case. Give us wisdom and keep us safe. She laid her head on her arms and prayed for wisdom concerning Brooks. She prayed for him and Katie. For healing and hope to bloom in their hearts. After she spent about thirty minutes in prayer, she rose from the altar steps and rubbed the small of her back.

She turned off her Wi-Fi, used her data package and hit the email icon on her phone to check her inbox. Sometimes she could get access to the internet and not a phone connection. *Please let this be one of those times.* It was. Opening the phone records, she hoped for something to pop.

Lonnie Kildare had made four calls within twenty-four hours before he was murdered.

All to the news station.

She sniffed. Was that…smoke she smelled? Panic bursting in her chest, she rushed to the front doors of the chapel. The doors wouldn't open. She put her weight into it, praying they would give, but she was barricaded in.

She sniffed again.

That was smoke. As she turned, she saw it.

Tongues of fire licking outside the windows. Her mouth turned to cotton as she stood, frozen. Fear gripping her and planting her feet to the floor.

The chapel was on fire. And she was locked inside.

She fumbled for her phone to call Brooks.

No service. Not even a bar.

She screamed out her frustration and fear. The smoke sifted into the chapel and the atmosphere became warmer.

Back door.

She sprinted through the small sanctuary to the back of the chapel. She lightly touched the door. The handle was hot to the touch.

Fire. Fire lurked outside the door. Using her coat as a glove, she placed it over the handle and pushed.

No go.

It had been secured too.

Andy? Had he sneaked out here and done this?

But the calls to the news station…

Finding those burner phones… She'd believed Ryan when he said he'd found them in Tracey's car. But she had no proof of that. Vera had been lured outside. To a place he knew had shoddy cell reception—that's why he called her from his car down the road.

The calls to the news station were to Ryan.

Somehow, he and Lonnie Kildare had a connection.

Ryan was obsessed with Tracey. Went everywhere with her. It wasn't a sicko who had felt a connection through the TV screen, but one who'd connected through the camera lens. Ryan had a firsthand show to see her in action as she reported those fires.

It wouldn't have been difficult to discover Andy had arrested Dominguez and Page. Ryan said he didn't want to be a cameraman forever. He had investigative ambition. May even want the spotlight, too, at some point. He could have done all the things she suspected Andy or Keegan of doing.

How was he connected with Lonnie Kildare though?

The sizzle and crackle of fire sent her heart into flight.

Now. She had to get out now!

FOURTEEN

Brooks sat at the kitchen table with a fresh cup of coffee. He'd considered going out to the chapel, but he didn't want to interrupt Vera's solace.

He noticed an email notification on his phone and opened it.

Lonnie Kildare's phone records? Had Vera sent for them and forgotten to tell him? That was odd.

He scrolled through and paused at the four calls within the twenty-four hours of Lonnie's death.

The news station? What in the world? What had Vera figured out and when?

Tracey entered the room. "What's going on?" she asked and cocked her head.

"Where'd you say Andy was again?"

"A walk."

Pieces began to connect. "Where's Ryan tonight?"

"I don't know. Why? What's going on?"

Brooks glanced at his phone again, a knot cording in his gut and his chest tightening. "Vera had Lonnie Kildare's phone records sent to us. He called the news station four times before he died."

"My news station?" She shook her head, squinted. "Are you saying Ryan knew Lonnie Kildare?"

Unbelievable. He'd been right under their noses. In his home. Near his daughter. "Would he have known the security code to the house?"

"It's possible. Whenever I punched in the numbers, I didn't hide it from him. But it can't be Ryan. I know Ryan. He was with me at all the fires."

"But he could have hired someone. Like Wiley Page and Sal Dominguez."

Outside the window, he caught a glimpse of smoke. "What in the world?" he muttered. His heart clenched. "I think the chapel's on fire!" He cried out to God and bolted from the living room. "Stay here with Katie! Call Andy. Send him to the chapel and call the fire department," he screamed as he raced out the back door.

Up ahead, flames touched the sky and the clouds billowed like dirty cotton balls. Vera! No. No. No. Fire engulfed the wooden chapel, the sounds of glass shattering in the heat chilled his spine. Flames devoured the roof.

Feeling utterly helpless, he raced around back, but it appeared this time that Ryan had lit the entire place instead of one point of entry. He caught sight of a gasoline can near the edge of the woods, confirming his suspicions. This time he'd made sure Vera couldn't escape.

"Vera!" he roared, but his voice sounded like a whisper against the raging fire. "God, help me find a way in!"

Vera shook and trembled. Pieces of the roof crashed down around her, and the heat was becoming unbearable. She had to find a way out.

Not fire. Not again.

Rushing into the hall, she burst into an old office, hunting for anything that might help her escape, but the smoke was creating too much darkness in the building and chaos in her heart. She coughed and sputtered and then paused. Was that…crying?

"Call out!" she hollered between coughs; her lungs clogged and burned. Inhaling became more difficult as the fire ate up the oxygen. "Call out!"

"It's me. It's Katie," the small voice cried.

The world slanted and Vera's head went dizzy. *No, not Katie.* "Where are you, baby?" she screamed.

"Under the desk."

Vera dropped to her knees and felt around until her hand contacted Katie's. She grabbed hold. "Crawl toward me." She coughed and gagged. "I'm gonna get you out of here." Somehow. No matter what, she had to make sure Katie lived. For Katie. For Brooks. For herself. "Grab ahold of my shirt and don't let go. We need to stay low."

Sweat rolled down her back and plastered her hair to her face and neck. Katie whimpered and coughed, but hung on and crawled along with her. Another side window exploded in the chapel area.

She found a wall and maneuvered Katie against it, then shrugged out of her coat and pressed it to Katie's face. "Keep this on your face. Don't move unless I tell you to. I'm going to find a way out."

Fire shot through the side windows, licked up the walls and consumed the roof. Stray pieces of wood cracked, popped and fell all around. The stage was fire-free and Vera spotted the rug. All she had to do was get Katie to safety. She couldn't worry about herself, but knowing what the fire felt like on skin—the searing, melting pain—sent a wave of nausea and a new round of fear into her. It was excruciating. Unbearable. Torture.

She would not let Katie experience that.

Scrambling, eyes burning and lungs on fire, she grabbed the rug and dragged it over to Katie then ran back and grabbed a folding chair from the small stage area. "Katie, listen to me. I'm going to roll you in this rug and then I'm going to get you out the front window. It was a tall slender window but hopefully just wide enough to fit Katie through. Once you hit the ground, you roll and roll and roll yourself out and run. Find your daddy."

By the time he found Vera, she'd likely have perished, but she couldn't think about that right now. Katie didn't speak. They were running out of precious time. Precious oxygen.

"Stand back," she demanded and swung the chair at the only window that hadn't already been engulfed in flames. One. Twice. Three times until the glass shattered. She used the chair to create an opening. The density of the rug would protect her from the glass and hopefully not be too bulky to get stuck.

"I can't do this," Katie cried.

"Yes, you can," she said with authority, and framed Katie's face. "You are brave. You are clever and you can do this. You roll and roll and roll yourself out then run and find your daddy. And tell him…you tell him Miss Vera loves him. Okay? I love him and… I love you." She choked on her words and hot tears leaked down her cheeks.

"Yes, ma'am. I love you, too, Miss Vera. I don't want to leave you."

"I know," she said as she eased her onto the rug and began rolling her up like a hotdog. "You're not leaving me. You're letting me let you go. No shame in that."

Once she had her rolled tightly, she swallowed hard. *God, what if she burns? Keep her from burning.*

She struggled to pick her up in her arms. The fabric scratched her face, but it was thick and tough on the bottom. Katie would be secure inside long enough to get out of harm's way.

A beam began to pop like thunder and she flinched. Time was short. Too short.

Now or never.

This chapel was about to collapse. "I love you, Katie Bug. Be good to your daddy. No more trouble." Flames danced along the edges of the broken window. It had to be now.

She swung her back and forth like a pendulum, gaining momentum with each swing, using strength she knew was not her own. With one last swing, Vera used all the force in her body and thrust Katie through. She sailed through the flames and out to safety. The child would be bruised and jarred—assuredly traumatized— but she'd live.

Vera's job was done. This was as far as she was meant to come.

She prayed the smoke would take her before the flames.

How in the world was Brooks going to get in there to Vera? The whole chapel was surrounded. A flash of movement caught his eye as he raced to the front of the chapel.

It was moving through the air.

The bottom was on fire.

He heard a voice. A scream!

Katie. *Oh, Katie!* He bolted for the mass on the ground. She was wrapped in the rug from the chapel. Moving quickly, he tugged off his sweatshirt and beat the flames at the corner of the rug. "I'm here, baby. I got you! I got you!" *Lord, please don't let her be burned.*

"Daddy!" she wailed and he caught a glimpse of the top of her hair. He finished unrolling the carpet and his baby girl was crying and covered in black soot. She fell against him, coughing. "Miss Vera is in there, Daddy! We have to get her out."

Vera. Vera had sacrificed herself for his daughter. Knowing it would likely seal her fate. How? How did he get in there? He grabbed the rug and draped it over his body. Where was the fire department? Where was Keegan? Where was Andy? Had Ryan set fire to his home too?

Too many thoughts. Too many fears.

"Stay here. You understand?"

"Daddy, you can't go in there. It's on fire!"

"I can't do nothing, Katie."

She nodded. "She said she loves you. Be careful. Please come out."

He raced toward the chapel, trying to find an entry point that wasn't consumed by flames. At the back of the chapel, he saw the old storm cellar door. He'd told Katie not to go down there with the snakes and critters and all sorts of things that might hurt her. But it might be useful now.

He put some muscle into it, ripped the door off the rusty hinges then tossed off the rug. He wasn't sure if he could get to the chapel from there, but he had to try. As he dove down inside, the smell of rot and must and earth hit his gag reflexes. Feeling along the walls, he scooted his way forward as his eyes adjusted.

The wall led to what felt like a ladder leading up into the chapel. He began to climb.

One of the wooden rungs gave way and he fell. He started again, being careful not to allow his weight to crush another rotten ladder rung.

His head hit something hard. He was at the top. Pushing on what felt like a door, he put all his strength into it. It wouldn't budge. It must have furniture over it. No one had needed it in years.

He pushed again, praying and screaming Vera's name.

But he knew she would never hear him over the roar of the fire.

She may not even be conscious.

Or alive.

No. He would not accept another woman he loved dying. "God, please help me. Help me save her. Help me free her." He pushed again and felt some give. Whatever was blocking the door had shifted. Again and again, he pushed, his breath coming in pants and sweat pouring from his brow and down his back, sticking his shirt to his skin.

Finally, the door rose slightly. No flames flooded the open crack. He shoved again with even more force, and the door lifted open. He was in the old office that had once been a bedroom for the reverend on the ranch. The heat was unbearable. The smoke black and blinding.

"Vera!" he bellowed and repeated her name. Soot invaded his throat and he gagged and coughed. "Vera!" He dropped to his knees and crawled his way out of the office, keeping to the wall so he wouldn't lose his sense of direction.

His hand touched something. He flinched then realized it was hair. Vera's hair. He felt until he could touch her face, feel her skin. Moving his fingers to her neck, he felt for a pulse.

She was alive!

"Vera," he called into her ear. Nothing. He scooped her limp body into his lap and scooted on his backside the way he'd come until he found the opening to the storm shelter. He turned on his stomach and slid to the ladder then moved down two rungs. He dragged Vera toward him then let her fall over his shoulder like a sack of potatoes, using his other hand to grip the side of the rickety wall ladder.

One rung.

Two.

Three.

His foot hit the fourth rung and it cracked. Brooks lost his balance and they fell from the ladder. He clung to Vera and took the brunt, his back hitting the old dirt-packed floor with a sickening thud, stealing his breath.

But they were alive. And safe.

For now.

Picking Vera up, he carried her to the cellar door and gently raised her up and out onto the ground, then he followed. They had to get away; the place was moaning and creaking like a dying animal.

Any minute it was going to come crashing down.

Lifting her into his arms, he sprinted around

the chapel toward the front. Katie was about a hundred yards away.

Andy stood near her and Tracey too. The fire unit was barreling across the yard to get to them, but the chapel was destroyed. They could only save the woods beyond before it reached the mountain brush.

As soon as he laid Vera on the ground, Katie ran toward them and dropped beside Vera. "Is she dead, Daddy?"

She lay limp and unmoving. Her face black with dirt and soot. Her clothes ripped and torn and burns on her hands. Not more burns. But they didn't look too bad.

Paramedics rushed to their side. Two went to work on Vera, one checked Katie and her vitals, and one saw to Brooks. He shoved the oxygen mask away as Keegan ran over, his team spraying the building and the woods beyond to saturate it before fire could kindle.

"What happened, Brooks?" Keegan asked.

"Ryan. Ryan did it." He might be long gone by now. But no matter how long it took, he would find him. Hunt him down and bring him to justice by locking him away forever.

Vera coughed and her eyes fluttered open. "Brooks...where...how... Katie?"

Of course her first thoughts would be of

Katie. Man, he loved this woman. Selfless. Fearless.

Katie knelt over her, an oxygen mask over her face. "Daddy saved you, Miss Vera." She coughed. "I told him you loved him. I think he loves you too." She grinned up at her dad and for the first time in a long time, he knew they were going to be okay.

Andy put a BOLO out on Ryan Peterson. Tracey's knees buckled and the paramedics tended to her. "It's over now," he said to her. "All we have to do is find him. And we will, Trace. We'll find him and put him away to rot in prison forever."

She nodded and leaned against Andy.

Brooks and Katie rode together in one ambulance and Vera rode in another, Tracey accompanying her so she wouldn't be alone.

Two hours later, a dose of antibiotics and Vera's hands wrapped, Andy drove them back to the ranch. Keegan was waiting. He followed them into the house. Once he was alone with Brooks, he said, "I'm sorry we couldn't save the chapel."

"What took you so long to get to us?"

"We got a call to another fire near Serenity Falls." That was on the far end of the town. "When we got there, nothing. Prank call. Then we got the call about your fire and it took us longer than it should have."

Ryan had purposely called the fake fire in to keep them away as long as possible to ensure Vera died. He'd had no way of knowing Katie had gone out there before Vera. She'd kept a stash of true crime books out there. Brooks would teach her a lesson in deceit later when he wasn't still shaken up at almost losing her. He'd be irritated then.

Right now, he had everyone he loved alive and together in one place.

"He used gasoline," Keegan explained. "Ran it around most of the chapel, dousing walls, windows and everything. If that cellar hadn't been there, Brooks…"

"I know," he murmured. Vera would have died. Now, she was resting in her room. Katie was with her, didn't want to leave her side. So far, there was no word on Ryan. Police said his drawers were tossed like he'd packed in a hurry to get out of town. Didn't matter. He could run but he could not hide.

"I'm gonna check on Vera and Katie." Leaving Keegan with Andy and Tracey in the kitchen, he strode down the hall to Vera's room. Her door was cracked and he peeked inside. She was propped up on pillows. Katie sat beside her, brushing Vera's hair.

"My dad's taking me on a trip once they catch Ryan."

"Oh yeah?" Vera said through a raspy voice. The smoke hadn't done any damage but it had affected her. Doc said her voice might be that way a week or two. "Where you gonna go?"

"Well, I've only had a globe for research, so I'm not sure. Where would you like to go?"

"Me?" Vera closed her eyes, clearly enjoying Katie tending her hair. "I'd like to visit Ireland. It's been a dream."

"I like their accents but I'm not sure I can do tripe. I read about that in social studies." Katie turned her nose up. "You want to stay in a big castle?"

"I do. How about you?"

"Yeah, that might be cool. But I also wanna do Disney."

Vera chuckled. "I hear ya."

Katie stopped brushing and faced Vera. "I never suspected him. I totally get it now. When neighbors of serial killers say how nice and normal they were. I even had a crush on him. But no worries, I won't be writing him letters in prison."

Vera cackled. "Good. I'd hate to find out and come whip your tail."

"I wish you didn't have go, Miss Vera. I think my dad loves you. And I'd be cool with that. I mean… I miss my mom. I wish she was here. But she's not. I think you could look out for him. Not like cooking dinners and stuff, although he'd probably appreciate it." She scrunched her nose. "But like you could totally protect him on the job. Watch his back. I'd… I'd trust you to do that since he's not gonna give up catching bad guys."

Vera touched Katie's cheek.

Brooks wiped the moisture from his eyes. His beautiful, rotten kid was the most mature, wonderful young woman he'd ever known. He was proud of her. Proud of who she was going to become. She had all the best parts of him and CeCe. She just needed to be molded, guided and encouraged.

"That means so much to me. But adults are more complicated than that."

"Why? I think it's pretty simple."

Childlike faith. He lightly knocked on the door and they both looked up. Vera smiled and Katie jumped off the bed. Oh, he hoped she didn't play matchmaker right now. She laid the brush on the dresser. "I'm gonna go spin my globe." She gave Brooks the eye. "After all that, I feel like I deserve at least one device back."

Brooks sighed. "We'll discuss it later."

"That's a fat no." She left the room and closed the door behind her.

Brooks splayed his hands in front of him. "It is a fat no. She sneaked out to read books I told her she couldn't. And she did steal AirPods, among other things." He crossed the room and sat beside Vera on the edge of the bed. Her fingers poked out of the bandages. She was pale and dark half moons had developed under her eyes. "How do you feel?"

"How much did you hear of that conversation?"

Busted.

"All of it," he murmured. He ran his index finger down her bandaged hand. "You scared me to death, Vera. But you—" he choked on his words, emotion clogging his throat and tightening his chest "—you were willing to die for my daughter." A tear leaked from his eye. He could care less about machismo. "You rolled her in a rug and threw her from a window to spare her life. I don't know how to thank you."

"I didn't do it for a thank-you. I didn't even do it because I took an oath to protect and serve. I did it because I love that kid. She's gonna be a world changer."

"Or a criminal mastermind." He laughed.

"Or that." She grinned then sobered. They held each other's gaze for one beat. Two. "Thank you. For saving me."

He brushed her hair from her face. She didn't

flinch. "Katie said you told her to tell me you love me."

Vera licked her lips.

"Knock, knock." Andy opened the door. "Hey, El Paso police found Ryan's car at a hotel. They checked with the management and he did check in, but they haven't found him. They're sitting on the place. He couldn't have gone far on foot."

"Good. We're close. I'll be glad when we have him. Find anything that would incriminate him at his place when you searched?"

Andy shook his head. "Nothing. Gas can in his shed, but that could be for a lawn mower."

"Thanks."

"You need anything else, let me know. I'm taking Tracey to her place to pack a few things she needs. She says she's going to work tomorrow. Not giving him the satisfaction of forcing her into hiding."

Brooks nodded. Andy saluted and left them.

"I want to talk to Lonnie Kildare's brother. He might know Ryan or be able to connect the two." She pushed out of the bed, clearly not wanting to get back to the subject they'd been discussing.

Loving each other.

"Where are you going?"

"To call him."

"Now? Vera, you need to rest. We can call first thing in the morning." She was using this as an excuse to not discuss her feelings. Why? Why was she balking?

"He might know Ryan and be able to help us find him. He left the hotel. Maybe someone picked him up. He's not an idiot. He knows we know it's him. That we're hunting him down. He's gotten away with so much. I also want a full background done on him. We'll find something in his past that points to this kind of behavior."

"Fine. But in the morning. Even I need a night to sleep. Or try to." And should he redirect their conversation? Had she changed her mind in the past four hours?

"Okay. I'll rest." She crossed her arms over her chest.

He shook his head. She was so stubborn. "Then I'll let you get to it."

At the door, she called his name. He turned back.

"I did tell Katie that, Brooks. Because I do. But I want to wrap this case up. Then we can… we can talk."

His heart soared. "I like that idea. Because I do, too, Vera. I do too."

He closed the door and felt like he was floating. Didn't matter how much his body ached or his head hurt. Vera loved him. And somehow they'd make it work.

He needed to talk to Katie. It was only fair and right. And he still wanted time away with her. That wasn't being pushed onto the back burner. Not now. Not ever.

FIFTEEN

Vera took a pain pill and moved pretty slowly this morning. Yesterday had been traumatic to say the least. She wasn't ready to have the *I love you* conversation. Not because she didn't want to, but she was bone-weary, on pain meds and feeling sore. She wanted to be well and in all her faculties. She wanted to catch Ryan Peterson and close the book on this debacle.

Brooks had gone into the station earlier and Katie was in her room reading a Nancy Drew book she'd checked out from the online library. Vera had heated them up frozen breakfast sandwiches, despite her bandaged and tender hands. Showering had been complicated. But she was now dressed and in the kitchen awaiting a pot of coffee that was brewing.

She'd left a voice mail for Lonnie Kildare's brother, Kenny. She'd also requested a full background on Ryan from her team at the BAU. They might be able to give her something more thorough than the local police. So far, she didn't see anything incriminating.

Ryan grew up in Gran Valle. Left to go to college at Baylor. Nothing on his college record. He appeared squeaky clean, but that didn't mean he was. Only meant he'd never been caught.

The coffeepot beeped and she poured a fresh cup. The sky was heavy and gray. Ash still floated along the air. The chapel had been beautiful. Maybe at some point Brooks could rebuild it. In memory of CeCe. Even put a little prayer garden next to it. A fleeting thought that she could put a little memento to Danny out there, too, zinged by.

She had herself moving here. Leaving the Bureau? The BAU? She loved being a federal agent. Loved profiling. Chelsey had left to move nearby. Duke had left and moved to West Texas too. Maybe they could open their own agency. Private consulting and profiling. She laughed, but it wasn't a terrible idea.

Her phone rang. Kenny Kildare. She answered. "Agent Vera Gilmore."

"Hi, Agent Gilmore. Kenny Kildare returning your call. I'm happy to help. I want my brother's killer caught and brought to justice, but I'm not sure I know any more now than I did six months ago."

Maybe true. Maybe not. "We believe we know

who killed your brother. But we can't seem to figure out the connection. The day your brother died, he made four phone calls to Serenity Canyon's local news station. Channel two. Did you or your brother know a Ryan Peterson?"

"Doesn't ring a bell with me, but that doesn't mean Lonnie didn't know him. Lonnie isn't a stranger to that area. He likes trips to Big Bend."

"So camping at Twisted Shoe wasn't odd?" It was remote.

"Maybe a little. Since it was so far out. All I know is he had a way to help the business. It was going under. He left. Then he died."

Could he have been coming to extort money from Ryan? Ryan had killed him and then to cover it up, he'd killed again—someone closer to Tracey. Then someone even closer to appear as if he was escalating. That made him a criminal genius. Except for the calls to the station. She'd pulled Ryan's private phone records. No calls from Lonnie to his cell. Maybe calling his place of work put pressure on Ryan, pressure to comply with Lonnie's request. "If I send you a picture over text, can you tell me if you recognize him?"

"Sure."

She had one from the park fire. Of Ryan and Tracey. She uploaded it and the swoosh sounded. "I just sent it."

"That him? This Ryan guy?" Kenny asked.

"Yeah."

"I don't know him. But... I definitely know her. That's Tracey Tisdale."

Wait. What? She pinched the bridge of her nose. "How do you know Tracey?"

He sighed. "She lived here in Lubbock. Nannied for us. My wife was killed in a car accident and she stayed on for a while, but I think... well, there was some misunderstandings and I had to let her go."

The room spun. "Did you say your wife was killed in a car accident? Can I ask how?"

"Tire blew." He sniffed. "About thirteen years ago."

Stomach knotting, she blew a heavy breath. "Did Lonnie know her?"

"Well, sure. He came over all the time. Occasionally, she babysat for all the kids when we double dated."

They had it wrong. So wrong. "How did she respond to your rejection? I'm assuming the misunderstanding was over romantic notions."

"Yeah," he said softly. "She didn't take it well. Kinda keyed my car and took a bat to it. Called me for weeks. One call she was sweet and apologizing, asking to get together for coffee. The next she was irate, irrational. Kinda scary."

"You take out a restraining order?"

"Yeah, and I found out it wasn't the first one taken out on her."

"It wasn't?"

"A buddy on the force did a check on her, and some guy had taken out a restraining order on her in college. Stalking and damage to his car. That's all I know. Once I told her I was going to take one out, too, I never heard from her again. Good riddance. I had a life to try and put back together."

One she'd wanted to be a part of. Two wives. Two tires blown. Two deaths. That was too much to chalk up to coincidence.

"Thank you, Mr. Kildare. If I need anything else, I'll be in touch." She ended the call and entered her password on her computer to search the database for Tracey Tisdale. There it was. One restraining order by a Chuck Chalmers. She clicked a few more keys and found a number then dialed it.

"Hello?" a deep male voice said after the fourth ring.

"Hi, Chuck Chalmers?"

"Yes," he said warily.

She told him who she was and why she was calling. "Anything you can tell me about Tracey would be helpful."

"Yeah, she's crazy. I'm happy to help."

"How do you know her?"

"She was in my Comp class in college. Then she started hanging out with my girlfriend, Erin. They became best friends. One weekend, they went to the lake for a girls' getaway and Erin drowned. Tracey was right by my side, which was cool at first. But then she got super clingy and I realized she wanted to be more than friends. Erin hadn't even been gone two months. I freaked out. We argued. She keyed my car and sliced my tires. Basically harassed me by phone and stalked me. My parents told me to get a restraining order, so I did. Eventually, I heard she transferred schools. Never heard or saw her again."

A drowning. "Was there ever any whiff of foul play?"

"No. We all thought it was an accident, even the cops. But after that crazy chick, I wondered. Sometimes, I still wonder."

Vera wasn't wondering. The pattern fit. Tracey was assuming women's identities by stepping into their roles after eliminating them. Who knew how many more victims Tracey had killed to steal their lives. "What's Erin's last name?"

"Sorkin. Why? Has Tracey killed someone? Did she kill Erin?" His voice rose and Vera hated to make him relive the pain. It was looking like she'd staged more than one murder.

"The investigation is ongoing but—" Tracey entered the kitchen, gun in hand and a finger to her lips for Vera to keep quiet. She motioned for her to end the call. "I'll be in touch if necessary. Thank you, Mr. Chalmers."

"No problem." He ended the call.

"Slide the phone across the island and don't try anything stupid," Tracey said. "Katie's in the bedroom and I'd hate for her to end up hurt." She used the gun to signal Vera to slide the phone. Vera complied.

"You set all this up."

"I had every intention of seeing Andy go down for this. His arrests. His burner phones. I wanted Ryan to see them. I knew he'd call you. Or maybe even Brooks. It was just a really good thing for me that he met you down at the chapel. I saw you two talking when Brooks assumed I was resting."

"And Katie?"

Tracey showed the first sign of remorse. "I didn't know Katie was in the chapel, but so what? Brooks was going to leave town with her. She was going to make him leave me. Another death would have only given me more opportunity to take care of him. See to his needs. Allow him a chance to fall further in love with me. I know he loves me. He just doesn't realize how much. I've been the one to pick up the pieces since CeCe died. I've been the number one around here. Until he called you."

"You killed Mr. Kildare's wife. Lonnie figured it out, didn't he? He dug into your past. Discovered Erin's drowning. He connected the dots then called to extort money because his business was going under. He could ruin your plans, so you found a junkie you could bribe with drugs or money, or something, and he torched the camper."

"No one is going to tell me what to do. I don't think he really had any evidence, but I didn't need him talking. Digging. So I agreed to pay him. I had no intentions of doing that." Venom pulsed in her eyes and her mouth hardened. "But I knew it would eventually come back to me. So I had to create a plan. I enlisted two of Andy's arrests. Junkies will do about anything for a fix. I promised fixes for their willingness to do what I needed."

Vera's phone rang. "Brooks." Tracey stepped closer, pocketed the phone. "You showed up and at first I thought no big deal, but then I saw the way Brooks looked at you. Heard him sing your praises on the TV. You were in the way from the start. I've worked years to be where I am. The moment I saw Brooks at the gym with CeCe… I knew he was special. She'd talked about her hunky detective husband. What a great man he was. A great father. He'd bought this ranch and they were fixing it up. I wanted that."

"You wanted to be CeCe. You wanted to be Erin Sorkin and you wanted to be Mrs. Kildare."

"It's not fair. I deserved Joan Kildare's life. I deserved CeCe's life. Erin's. My dad was a lousy drunk and my mom couldn't care less about me. I had nothing. They had everything. People who loved them. Money. Homes. Friends."

"You're sick. And you're selfish."

"Maybe. But I'm going to be Brooks's wife. Katie's mom. Not you."

"You're going to shoot me here in the kitchen?" Fear licked at her veins but she held it together, remained cool and calm—at least on the outside.

"No. Not here. I think maybe you're going to leave a note that it's time for you to go back to Quantico. And you're going to have an accident. It'll hurt Brooks. But I'll be here to help him grieve. Women that get in my way get theirs."

The intern. Tracey had felt threatened in her job. Katie's soccer coach had Katie's affection. She'd had to die. Vera was right. It wasn't about fires. It was about people getting in Tracey's way of having what she wanted.

She was unhinged. Sociopathic.

"Out the back door. Slowly." Tracey kept her gun trained on Vera. She would kill her. Without thought. But how would she get around the fact that Ryan hadn't killed anyone? And eventually Brooks would talk to Kenny Kildare and discover the truth himself.

The truth that Tracey had met CeCe and coveted her life. Her man. Her family. And she'd murdered her just like she'd killed Joan Kildare. Brooks had blamed himself for CeCe's death, and so had Katie. But it wasn't his fault. The tires may have needed to be changed but that hadn't meant they would have blown and sent CeCe over the edge. Tracey had helped it along. Probably knowing the tires needed to be changed. No one had investigated it as a suspicious death.

Vera's heart broke for Brooks. The unnecessary guilt. The unforgiveness.

She opened the back door and slowly stepped onto the porch. "Where are we going?"

"For a ride. In your rental."

She had to comply for now. Katie was in danger. Tracey wouldn't think twice about killing her. All her love and affection were nothing more than show. She was playing a part. She had no remorse. No empathy.

She'd created a stalker so Brooks would keep her close. Protect her. Fall in love with her. She probably would end up killing Andy in false self-defense. He'd forever be known as a se-rial killer.

But if Ryan wasn't a part of this, why had he run?

As she reached the car, Brooks barreled into the drive, back from the station. His arrival mo-mentarily distracted Tracey. Vera turned to jab her in the face and disarm her, but Tracey got the jump and put her in a headlock, the gun to her head. "I'm not going to prison and I'm not going to die. Can't say the same for you."

Brooks bounded from the truck. His hands up in surrender, his gun on his hip, as he inched slowly toward them. "Tracey, what is going on?"

"I did it for us, Brookie."

He squinted, confused. She'd used Vera's pet name for him. She was now attempting to as-sume her identity.

Brooks's heart pounded and a million thoughts raced through his brain. Why was Tracey hold-ing Vera at gunpoint? "Let's talk about this, Trace."

"Brookie, do you remember the first time we met?" Tracey asked, her voice soft and sugary.

First time they'd met? No. Not really. He had a sick feeling if he told her that, she'd go off the deep end. "Do you?"

"Of course. I'd seen CeCe at the gym a few

times and one day you came in to bring her headphones. She'd forgotten them. You kissed her and then you looked up and saw me on the treadmill. I was running a marathon."

He remembered bringing CeCe the headphones. That wasn't the first time. But he didn't remember seeing Tracey.

"We made a connection. I knew you wanted me. And I wanted you. But...she was in the way. So I did what I had to do. I became her friend. Everything she ever wanted. Bestest of the best. I even went to church with her. To the women's retreat."

What was she saying? What was happening right now? Vera's profile hit him with force. Obsessive. Stalker. Likely had a pattern of this behavior.

She'd been fixated on him.

She'd left the retreat early. Driven separately. His knees turned to water. No. No.

"I was getting everything in order," Tracey said. "Katie loves me. We could be together. Andy would be out of the way."

Red spotted his eyes and he clenched his jaw. "Did you kill my wife?"

"You wanted to be with me. Why didn't you change her tires? You knew what could happen. I just helped it happen sooner. So we could be together."

It took everything in his power not to rush her and strangle her with his bare hands or shoot her. How could he have not seen she was off her rocker?

"But then this one showed up and messed everything up. I had to fix it. But she refuses to die. You don't want this." She sneered. "You've seen what's underneath the long sleeves and pants." Her snarl curdled his blood. "It's hideous. You can't deny that. Can he?" she hissed in Vera's ear.

Vera's eyes shimmered with moisture and, for the first time ever, he saw Tracey's true nature.

She was hideous. Repugnant. Inhuman.

"Do you think he can bear those ugly marks?" she said to Vera and shoved the gun harder against her head.

"No," Vera breathed. "I can barely stand them. I broke every mirror in my bathroom. I wouldn't blame him for rejecting me."

Brooks's chest cracked wide open but he couldn't voice the truth. That Vera was beautiful. Every inch. Every part. Inside and out.

"See? We can be together, Brooks. You, me and Katie. Go away on that trip. Ryan, Andy—either of them can take the fall. I don't care." Her voice hardened. "But she's got to go."

Vera strained against the muzzle of the gun to her head. Her hands were badly burned or she'd have disarmed her by now. She had handled grown men attacking her. She could handle Tracey. If she wasn't injured.

"Tracey, think this through." Brooks inched closer not pulling his gun. Tracey was unhinged and if he pointed a gun on her, Vera would be dead before he aimed.

"We find Andy. We say we discovered it was Andy framing Ryan. With her brains, Vera figured it out, but Andy shot and killed her and you shot Andy. Or I did. Self-defense. They'll believe us," she urged.

She was certifiable. Delusional.

And she was going to do it. She was going to pull the trigger; it was in her glazed, hollow eyes.

Suddenly, she was knocked back, the gun tumbling from her hands, and Vera spun on her, mouth agape. She kicked the gun away and Brooks pounced on her. Lying next to her was one of Katie's practice arrows. She'd used it to knock the gun from her hands. Brooks whipped his head around and his daughter stood in her shooting position.

"Katie?" His twelve-year-old brave girl had just rescued the woman he loved. The woman he loved had rescued Katie. And him in so many ways.

"Aren't you glad I begged for those lessons?

Maybe you'll rethink my grounding." She gave him a smug grin but fear pulsed in her eyes and her hands tremored. She'd been a crack shot. Those lessons had paid off. He cuffed Tracey and left her with Vera, rushing and scooping Katie into his arms.

"You are no longer grounded."

"That's a start." She hugged him and laid a big ole kiss on his cheek, like when she was little. Man, he missed her sweet baby-girl love.

Vera spoke up, strong and steady. "Tracey Tisdale, you're under arrest. For the murder of CeCe Brawley, Lonnie Kildare, Wendy Siller, Adrianna Montega, Wiley Page and Sal Dominguez."

"I didn't kill Wiley Page."

"My mistake." She finished Mirandizing her and Brooks called 9-1-1. "And if they can find new evidence, maybe you'll go away for Erin Sorkin's drowning, too."

Katie laid her head on his shoulder and fell to pieces then. "She killed Mama."

"I know, baby." Brooks cried with her. They were going to grieve this time with one another.

Sirens wailed in the distance.

Police took Tracey into custody and took statements. The next few hours were a whirlwind. By midnight, they'd tracked down Ryan. He'd known Andy would find out about him and try to kill him. He'd truly believed Andy was the killer. Fearing for his life, he'd gotten out of town until it blew over, having no clue he'd become a wanted man.

Andy *had* been on a walk the night of the chapel fire. Tracey had sneaked out of her room in the house, stolen the gas can from the barn and set the chapel on fire.

It had seemed like forever till they got it all settled, and now Katie was finally in bed and asleep.

Brooks entered the living room. Vera sat on the sofa in complete silence, bathed in the soft light of the lamp beside her. Everything had happened at such a rapid pace they hadn't had time to talk and there was so much to say.

He eased down beside her.

"I'm sorry, Brooks. I'm so sorry you've felt responsible for CeCe's death and you weren't. I imagine you're grieving all over again. You and Katie. You need time. I booked a flight just now. I'm leaving in the morning. When you've had time, if you haven't changed your mind—"

He cut her off with his lips. All he'd wanted to do since Tracey was taken away was to kiss Vera. To feel her in his arms. To show her how much he loved her. Nothing Tracey said or did had deterred him from how he felt about her.

He'd talked to Katie. Had her full blessing.

Tenderly, carefully, cautiously, he kissed her. She melted into him and returned it with the same hope and love he was showing her.

"I love you," he murmured against her mouth. "I want to be with you." He slowly raised the sleeves on her sweater, revealing her scars. "These are not hideous. They are not repulsive. They don't define you, Vera. They're marks of courage and sacrificial love. When I see your scars, I'm reminded of Jesus's scars from His sacrificial love for us. And not just your scars, Vera. But the way you live and love others."

Tears ran down her cheeks. "I never saw it like that."

"You've been believing lies about yourself. But they are lies. Please, Vera. Let me love you. All of you. I meant it when I said I wasn't scared."

"I love you, Brooks. I do. So much. I just don't want you to feel ashamed of me."

"I could never." He framed her face. "I am proud to be with you and if you'll say yes, I'd be proud to call you my wife."

Wide-eyed and mouth agape, she gasped. "You want to marry me?"

"I can't say I regret our choice to take separate roads. I loved CeCe and I wouldn't trade Katie for anything. But I wanted to marry you once before. Thought we were going to spend our lives together. We have a second chance now and I want it."

"What about our jobs? And time with Katie? And—" He closed his lips over hers and this time he kissed her with more fervor, making his point about how much he loved her.

"We'll figure it out. As long as we're together, we can figure it out."

"Then my answer is yes. I never thought I'd marry again and to be married to a man I once wanted to say I do to…that can only be God."

"I'm gonna make you happy."

"You already do."

EPILOGUE

Three weeks later

Vera stood on the porch of the ranch as Brooks's truck rumbled up the drive. After he'd proposed, he and Katie had taken a two-week trip to Disney and then spent a week camping and hiking in Big Bend. They'd frozen their tails off but loved every minute, from the phone calls they'd had, which had been far and few between. It had been their time. To grieve. To reconcile what had actually happened to CeCe. And while they were off having daddy-daughter time, Vera had done some soul-searching of her own and made a few phone calls.

She'd pitched the idea to Chelsey Banks-Holliday and Duke Jericho about starting up a private firm. They could keep their jobs while they got it off the ground, she'd proposed. Vera still had a large amount of money from Danny's death she could invest and live off of while laying the groundwork.

Yesterday she'd gotten a call from them both to meet for lunch. Earlier today, they'd accepted her proposal to open up their own profiling and detective agency. They were going to be based out of Gran Valle for now. It was the closest to them. Further from Vera, but in time they might be able to open more offices in locations all over Texas.

They'd yet to come up with a good name. But they had time to mull it over. She hadn't been able to relay the news to Brooks yet. She'd flown in late last night and he'd been gone all morning. Katie had been at Allyson's, spending her first night back with her best friend.

Katie bounded from the truck and ran right into her arms. "I missed you and I got you a present."

"Is it a true crime book?"

"No, we lived that. Hey, we should write one! That would be sweet." Oh, this kid. "It's in my room. Wait here." She darted into the house.

Brooks took his time, a slow swagger as he kept his eyes on her, and finally ate up the distance between them. Her stomach dipped. "You're a sight for sore eyes. I've missed you." He drew her into his arms, his strong, warm chest brushing hers. He dipped his head and let her know with his kiss just how much he'd missed her.

"I missed you too. I have something to tell you."

"Yeah? You want to tell me now or open your present?" His smirk was playful and his eyes held mischief.

"Present. As long as it's not Minnie Mouse ears."

He chuckled and her heart soared. She wasn't sure if grown women were supposed to feel giddy over a man, but she did.

Brooks dipped on his knee and her throat turned dry and her heartbeat sped up.

"I know I asked you to marry me. But I thought I'd do it right." He held out a black-velvet box and opened the lid.

She sucked her bottom lip between her teeth and looked down at a gorgeous emerald-cut solitaire set in gold. She gasped at its beauty.

"Vera Gilmore, will you marry me? I love you so much."

"Yes," she breathed, light-headed, tears blurring her vision.

Brooks placed the ring on her finger and stood, then kissed her again.

A clearing of a throat drew their attention. Katie stood there grinning. "My gift." She handed her a box. A bigger box.

She opened it and grinned then laughed. A snow globe of Ireland. A big castle inside. "I love this."

"I know. And Dad's taking you for your honeymoon!"

"Katie! That was a surprise." Brooks frowned but his eyes danced.

"Sue me. That's what you get for asking a twelve-year-old to keep a secret." She shrugged and embraced Vera. "PS. I helped picked out the ring. You can thank me later."

"Katie!" Brooks laughed and put his arms around each of them and hugged them to him. "My girls. Life is never going to be dull around here."

Nor was it going to be lonely. Vera's heart was full. Her future was dazzling. As they chattered and headed for the kitchen, she thanked God for being so good and for orchestrating second chances. It hadn't been smooth but it had been worth it. Her scars told a story and maybe she could use them to help others.

"Hey," Brooks said and kissed her brow, "have I mentioned how much I love you?"

"Yes, but you can tell me again."

He leaned closer and whispered in her ear. "I'll be telling you as long as I live."

* * * * *

*If you enjoyed this Quantico Profilers story,
be sure to pick up the previous books in
Jessica R. Patch's miniseries:*

Texas Cold Case Threat
Cold Case Killer Profile

*Available now from
Love Inspired Suspense!*

And don't miss

A Cry in the Dark
*by Jessica R. Patch, a full-length suspense
from Love Inspired Trade,
available March 2023!*

Dear Reader,

We all have scars. Some are more easily seen. Don't let them hold you back and keep you hidden. They tell a story and your story is important. Someone needs to hear it. I'm so thankful for the scars of Jesus. They are beautiful and brave. Just like yours.

I love to share fun book news and more spiritual encouragement with readers, so please sign up for my monthly newsletter to get "Patched In" at www.jessicarpatch.com and connect with me on BookBub!

Jessica

Get 4 FREE REWARDS!

We'll send you 2 FREE Books plus 2 FREE Mystery Gifts.

FREE
Value Over
$20

Both the **Love Inspired®** and **Love Inspired® Suspense** series feature compelling novels filled with inspirational romance, faith, forgiveness and hope.

YES! Please send me 2 FREE novels from the Love Inspired or Love Inspired Suspense series and my 2 FREE gifts (gifts are worth about $10 retail). After receiving them, if I don't wish to receive any more books, I can return the shipping statement marked "cancel." If I don't cancel, I will receive 6 brand-new Love Inspired Larger-Print books or Love Inspired Suspense Larger-Print books every month and be billed just $6.49 each in the U.S. or $6.74 each in Canada. That is a savings of at least 16% off the cover price. It's quite a bargain! Shipping and handling is just 50¢ per book in the U.S. and $1.25 per book in Canada.* I understand that accepting the 2 free books and gifts places me under no obligation to buy anything. I can always return a shipment and cancel at any time by calling the number below. The free books and gifts are mine to keep no matter what I decide.

Choose one: ☐ **Love Inspired**
Larger-Print
(122/322 IDN GRHK)

☐ **Love Inspired Suspense**
Larger-Print
(107/307 IDN GRHK)

Name (please print)

Address   Apt. #

City   State/Province   Zip/Postal Code

Email: Please check this box ☐ if you would like to receive newsletters and promotional emails from Harlequin Enterprises ULC and its affiliates. You can unsubscribe anytime.

Mail to the **Harlequin Reader Service:**
IN U.S.A.: P.O. Box 1341, Buffalo, NY 14240-8531
IN CANADA: P.O. Box 603, Fort Erie, Ontario L2A 5X3

Want to try 2 free books from another series! Call 1-800-873-8635 or visit www.ReaderService.com.

---

*Terms and prices subject to change without notice. Prices do not include sales taxes, which will be charged (if applicable) based on your state or country of residence. Canadian residents will be charged applicable taxes. Offer not valid in Quebec. This offer is limited to one order per household. Books received may not be as shown. Not valid for current subscribers to the Love Inspired or Love Inspired Suspense series. All orders subject to approval. Credit or debit balances in a customer's account(s) may be offset by any other outstanding balance owed by or to the customer. Please allow 4 to 6 weeks for delivery. Offer available while quantities last.

Your Privacy—Your information is being collected by Harlequin Enterprises ULC, operating as Harlequin Reader Service. For a complete summary of the information we collect, how we use this information and to whom it is disclosed, please visit our privacy notice located at corporate.harlequin.com/privacy-notice. From time to time we may also exchange your personal information with reputable third parties. If you wish to opt out of this sharing of your personal information, please visit readerservice.com/consumerchoice or call 1-800-873-8635. **Notice to California Residents**—Under California law, you have specific rights to control and access your data. For more information on these rights and how to exercise them, visit corporate.harlequin.com/california-privacy.

LIRLIS22R3

THE 2022 LOVE INSPIRED CHRISTMAS COLLECTION

Buy 3 and get 1 FREE!

May all that is beautiful, meaningful and brings you joy be yours this holiday season...including this fun-filled collection featuring 24 Christmas stories. From tender holiday romances to Christmas Eve suspense, this collection has it all.

YES! Please send me the **2022 LOVE INSPIRED CHRISTMAS COLLECTION** in Larger Print! This collection begins with ONE FREE book and 2 FREE gifts in the first shipment. Along with my FREE book, I'll get another 3 Larger Print books! If I do not cancel, I will continue to receive four books a month for five more months. Each shipment will contain another FREE gift. I'll pay just $23.97 U.S./$26.97 CAN., plus $1.99 U.S./$4.99 CAN. for shipping and handling per shipment.* I understand that accepting the free books and gifts places me under no obligation to buy anything. I can always return a shipment and cancel at any time. My free books and gifts are mine to keep no matter what I decide.

☐ 298 HCK 0958   ☐ 498 HCK 0958

Name (please print)

Address   Apt. #

City   State/Province   Zip/Postal Code

> Mail to the **Harlequin Reader Service:**
> **IN U.S.A.:** P.O. Box 1341, Buffalo, NY 14240-8531
> **IN CANADA:** P.O. Box 603, Fort Erie, ON L2A 5X3
